Plea Of The Damned 1
Forgive Me Lucy

Plea Of The Damned 1
Forgive Me Lucy

Avril Sabine

Cracked Acorn Productions
Australia

Plea Of The Damned 1: Forgive Me Lucy

Published by
Cracked Acorn Productions
PO Box 1365
Gympie, Queensland 4570
Australia

978-1-925131-36-9 (Kindle)

978-1-925131-73-4 (EPUB)

978-1-925131-37-6 (Print)

Genre: Young Adult Urban Fantasy/Paranormal

*For everyone who has ever made a mistake
and wanted to take it back the moment it was
made.*

Plea Of The Damned

Have you ever done something and immediately wished you could undo it? Jack knows that feeling very well. He's damned, bound to haunt his old school and help students until he atones for his sins. It's the last thing he wants to do. But since the alternative is an eternity in hell, he's not about to say no.

Book 1: Forgive Me Lucy

Each afternoon when Lucy has arrived home from school she's found a white rose on her doorstep. Most people would be thrilled to have a secret admirer. She had been for a while, but it's become annoying not knowing who's leaving them. And if that wasn't bad enough, she now has a ghost wanting to know how he can help her. She doesn't have a problem and has no idea why he's pestering her. She's absolutely certain he's got the wrong person.

*

This story was written by an Australian author using Australian spelling.

Chapter One

Jack

Jack Richards sloshed whiskey into his empty glass, some of it ending up on the kitchen bench. He ran his hand across the bench to mop up the spill and only managed to smear the liquid further. After throwing back the contents of the glass he wiped the back of one hand across his mouth as he slammed the glass on the bench.

"Happy birthday," he muttered as he poured another shot, his hip supporting him against the edge of the kitchen cabinet where he slouched. "Happy eighteenth son, now get your backside down to the factory. I've talked to my boss for you." He drained the glass again and stared inside it. Throwing it over his shoulder he grinned in satisfaction at the sound of breaking glass as he raised the nearly empty bottle to his lips. "As if it were my fondest dream to be like my old man." He pushed away from the bench, weaving towards the doorway into the living room. He grabbed the doorframe he collided with. "Art school ain't for pansies."

His eyes zeroed in on the radio. He stumbled towards it and turned it on. The sound of Frank Ifield filled the room singing 'The Lovesick Blues'. Jack glared at the radio and changed the station. He swore when he heard 'Return To Sender' by Elvis Presley. He savagely yanked the radio cord from the wall and hurled the offending object across the room. The sound of the radio colliding with the wall followed by the sound of breaking glass brought Jack across the room to kneel in front of his mother's wedding portrait, now lying on the ground with the broken radio.

"No." He lifted the portrait, shaking glass from the frame. "No." The word was a wounded moan as he ran his finger over the scratch the glass had made in his mother's face. She looked so young. His age when she'd married her husband. Her veil had been borrowed from her best friend since lace had been hard to come by in 1944. Her rich brown hair was a cloud around her face as it fell to her shoulders, looking as black as his in the black and white photograph. Dark eyes looked off to the right and a smile was about to form. The scratch ran across one of her eyes. The eyes he'd inherited. He pressed the portrait to his chest as he rocked back and forth. Just like Rose, she'd left him too.

It had been all about the queen the past few months. Queen Elizabeth II due to arrive next week. It was all anyone talked about. Who cared about the Queen? The only Elizabeth he cared about was dead and buried. He pulled the portrait away from his chest to stare at the picture of his mother. Dead and buried. He stumbled to his feet, using his left hand to push himself up, barely noticing the glass that cut him and caused a slow drip of blood to fall on the flowered carpet.

A drink. That's what he needed. And a cigarette. He found the bottle where he'd left it in the kitchen, but he was out of cigarettes. He'd have to get some. He placed the portrait carefully on the bench.

"I'm sorry, Mum. I didn't mean to break your radio." He ran his finger over the scratch, staring at her damaged eye. The radio had been a birthday present. She'd liked to listen to music and her serials while she did the housework. Her last birthday present. She'd only been able to enjoy it a few months before she was gone. Stolen from him. Pain filled him and he reached again for the bottle. It didn't help. The pain remained. A cigarette. That's what he needed.

He paused halfway out of the room. He'd have to pass the school. The school and Rose. And Arthur. His hands became fists. It was all Arthur's fault. He'd been after Rose for years. He wasn't going to let him keep her. Rose was his. He was sick of losing people in his life. She might not be dead, but Rose might as well be for all the attention she paid him.

Jack straightened his shoulders. He was going to get her back and there was nothing Arthur could do to stop him. He strode towards his father's bedroom. Not if Arthur wanted to see another day.

Chapter Two

Jack

Jack paused at the door to the classroom, a nearly full bottle of whiskey dangling from his left hand, dried blood leaving a crust on his palm. The classroom was nearly empty. Rose stood with her hands on her hips as she glared at the banner. Wet paint glistened in the afternoon light coming through the window. He smiled as her lips puckered and one hand left her hip so her forefinger could tap against them, a slight frown forming between her brows.

"It has to be perfect."

Arthur reached out to brush his hand across her hair where it fell in long blond locks down her back. "It is. The Queen will love it. She won't notice any other banner."

Rage filled Jack and he reached for the gun in the

waistband of his jeans, hidden by his leather jacket. The first of March might be a warm day, but these days he didn't go anywhere without his jacket. He didn't care what people said. No one had the right to tell him how to dress. As he stepped into the classroom the other occupant reached out a hand to slip it around Rose's waist.

"It's perfect, Rose." Kay tilted her head to bump it against Rose's shoulder momentarily and brown locks mingled with blond. "You're a natural artist. We wouldn't expect anything else."

It had been what had first brought him and Rose together. Their art. He stepped further into the room and when they turned to see who entered, he spoke. "I want to talk to you, Rose. Get rid of them." He waved the gun towards each side of her.

Kay screeched, both hands covering her mouth. Her blue eyes were so wide the whites were unnaturally noticeable.

"Now listen here." Arthur stepped forward to shield the two girls.

"Shut your mouth. Another word from you and I'll shut it permanently." Jack turned his glare from Arthur to Kay when she gave another screech. "And that goes for you too." He had a swig from his bottle, his mouth dry. What was he doing here? He couldn't remember what thought process had brought him to this classroom. Then his gaze returned to Arthur and anger rushed through him.

"Jack." Rose stepped forward and away from her companions. "Why don't you put that bottle down and hand me the gun? It's your birthday. It's not every day your birthday falls on a Friday." Her lips curved into a smile, but it didn't reach her eyes. She held out a hand. "Please, Jack."

"You're always going on about how much I drink." Jack had another mouthful. He needed a cigarette, but they were tucked into the sleeve of his t-shirt and his hands were already full. If he put the bottle down Rose would think it was because she'd asked. He frowned. Why had he come? It took a moment. His birthday. "You said we'd go out together on my birthday." He gestured towards Arthur with the gun. "Before he stole you."

"We could still go somewhere. Tonight. There's all sorts of celebrations this weekend. Everyone's excited to have Queen Elizabeth coming to Brisbane." Rose took a hesitant step forward, her tone soothing. She let her hand drop to her side.

"Enough! I don't want to hear another word about the blasted queen." A movement behind Rose drew his attention and he saw Arthur throw himself forward. There was confusion as the sound of the gun rang out. Kay screamed and fainted. Blood blossomed on Arthur's shoulder as he slumped to the ground.

"No!" Rose threw herself at Arthur, pressing her hand against the flowing blood, sobs breaking free as she called his name.

His eyes fluttered. "Rose." Then he went limp.

"Arthur. Oh, Arthur." One hand went to his heart while the other was kept pressed against the wound. She turned her face up to Jack. "Please. You must call for an ambulance. Please."

Jack shook his head, the gun held at his side, pointed at the floor. "It was his own fault. He shouldn't have rushed me. This wasn't a game of footy."

"Jack. Please."

"No."

"You can't do this. Every time someone says the name Elizabeth you lose your temper. It's been more than a year. You have to let her go." Rose continued to hold her hand against Arthur's shoulder. "Please, Jack."

He shook his head. "Leave him be, Rose. You're mine. You told me you'd always be mine."

"That was before you started drinking and smoking and hanging out with the wrong people.

And that motorcycle. You can't expect a lady to ride on a motorcycle."

"Leave him be, Rose." He reached out and grabbed her arm, dragging her to her feet. "Leave. Him. Be."

Rose stared up at him, her gaze colliding with his, her voice whisper soft. "Please. Let me go."

Jack shook his head. "I can't. Not you too. I just can't."

"I'm sorry." She relaxed against him, one arm going around his waist, the other creeping inside his jacket.

"Rose?" Her body felt so familiar against his. It had been months since he'd held her like this. The bottle dropped from his hand and his arms went around her, the side of the gun pressed against the small of her back. "Rose." The word was a sigh as he closed his eyes, resting his chin against the top of her head. He felt her hand move further inside his jacket.

"I did love you. I thought we'd be together forever."

The sound of a pocket knife snapping open made him pull back to stare down at his own blade pressed against his chest. "Rose?"

"You scare me." Her hand trembled. "You won't stop following me. And now Arthur." She glanced over her shoulder to where he lay, blood spreading around him. Further over Kay was still unconscious on the floor. "You have to let me go. Please. Just let me go. Walk away."

Jack shook his head. "No. We're going. Now. Just the two of us. We're going to find somewhere no one can take you from me."

"No." Rose struggled wildly as Jack tried to drag her from the classroom. Her struggles drove the knife into flesh and the gun fired again. Her mouth opened wide as her eyes were drawn to the knife. Then her gaze slowly rose to meet Jack's, her mouth still open.

The gun fell to the ground and Jack reached for Rose, his eyes drawn to the blood soaking through the material of her dress, staining her middle. "Rose?" He reached out a hand and staggered, looking down at the knife that protruded from him. He frowned, not feeling anything. His knees buckled and collided with the ground as Rose dropped with him, her hands pressed against her stomach as she tried to rise. "I love you." His words were filled with confusion.

"I'm scared."

He tried to reach out to her. Comfort her. Promise he'd be there. No words came as he crashed to the ground, his head connecting with the floorboards. He could see the edge of Rose's dress, blood reaching the hem to pool on the wooden floorboards where she knelt. Behind her Arthur stretched out. His vision blurred and he saw his mother bending towards him. Going to her knees as she reached for him, tears streaking her face. "Forgive me." He spoke to his mother, but Rose answered instead.

"Never." The sound of her body hitting the floor filled the room.

He tried to call out to Rose, but words again failed him. Behind his mother he saw a winged man. He stood tall, a comforting hand resting on his mother's shoulder as she sobbed.

"Elizabeth. Let him go." The words were firm, but compassionate.

"He's my baby. There must be something I can do."

The angel shook his head. "He chose his own path."

"He lost his way and couldn't find the path." Elizabeth caressed Jack's cheek. "You heard him." She turned her head to the angel, her hand still on Jack. "At the end. You heard my son. He asked for forgiveness. He repented at the end. You must give him a chance."

The angel stared down at Elizabeth. Jack watched them both, the sound of his fading heartbeat filling his ears with its last desperate beats. He nearly missed the angel's reply over the noise.

"The usual plea of the damned." He nodded sharply. "He'll have his chance. For seven times seven years he shall be bound to this place forced to see and hear, but never be seen or heard. To never touch or feel, to be unforgiven by all who remember him. Then he shall have his chance to redeem himself."

"Thank you. You'll see. He won't disappoint me. I have complete faith he'll do all in his power to redeem himself. But what you said isn't true. I forgive him. Like my love he has it without asking. He's my son. Both are unconditional."

The angel gave another short nod then reached out his hand to her.

"Please. Let me stay with him to the end."

The angel continued to hold out his hand. "It is the end, Elizabeth. It's time to say goodbye."

Jack's eyes closed and he felt his mother's lips press against his forehead. He wanted to say something. Anything. No words came.

Elizabeth's hand cupped his cheek. "I know, baby. I love you too. I'll be waiting for you." Her lips pressed against his forehead again. "No matter how long it takes. I'll be waiting for you."

Chapter Three

Jack

Jack tapped his half empty packet of cigarettes against his drawn up knee. He'd nearly thrown them away numerous times, but there were so few things he could touch and feel that he hadn't been able to get rid of them. If only he'd managed to hang onto the bottle that day. What he wouldn't give for a drink. He winced as a group of girls passed the tree he leaned against, screeching and squealing excitedly. Make that several drinks. He tapped the packet against his knee one last time before he slid it into the sleeve of his t-shirt.

Yet another birthday. More than forty-nine years had passed since the angel had sentenced him to remain at the school for seven times seven years. Obviously angels couldn't count. Stuck enduring his eighteenth all over again. But without all the screw ups. How many times had he wished he could do that day over? He'd lost count. Far too many times. He sighed as he rose to his feet. What was the point of this? Wandering the same school day after day. It hadn't taken him long to realise that hell wasn't fire and brimstone. It was decades of sheer boredom.

How many years were they going to ignore him? Forever? "What was that overgrown bird thinking ditching me here?"

"That you'd have time to reflect on your sins."

Jack swore as he spun to face the angel he hadn't seen for more than forty-nine years. "And I couldn't have done that in less time? And what had happened to only forty-nine years? Can't you count?"

"You're lucky it wasn't longer. There was a great deal of disagreement over whether or not you deserved a chance at redemption. And no, you couldn't have reflected on your sins in a shorter time frame. Not and have it sink in. Especially since a lot of those first few years were spent cursing everyone and demanding attention." The angel grinned. "After the initial shock wore off you were worse than a two-year-old having a temper tantrum."

"I needed to know what happened to Rose."

"She certainly wasn't headed where you were."

"But she killed me."

"Self-defence is a different matter altogether. Now enough worrying about the sins of others. We need to discuss the atonement of yours."

Jack's eyes narrowed as he stared warily at the angel. "Atonement?"

The angel nodded. "For every single sin. No matter how minor."

What did angels consider sins? There were the obvious ones, like lying and the midnight auto supply. He was pretty certain the bible mentioned something about not stealing. It was also very clear about murder being a sin. Thou shalt not kill. You couldn't get much clearer than that. And he certainly had two counts of murder to deal with. He guessed he should be grateful it hadn't been three. But what about Chinese fire drills? Were they a sin? They'd only been a bit of a blast. Nothing much to get cut up over. He should probably add all the lies to the list. He didn't want to think about how many he'd told his father. In the end he'd stopped talking to him and left Frank to try and maintain communications on his own. He sighed. He guessed he'd better get started on the atonement business. It was probably going to take a while.

"What do I have to do?"

"You'll be assigned people who are in need of help and guidance."

Jack stared at the angel. "I'll be what?"

The angel smiled slightly. "You heard clearly."

"Guidance! Did you forget you're talking to a major screw up? I barely made it to my eighteenth birthday. And look what a stuff up I made of that."

"You've had years to figure out where you went wrong and what you should have done."

"More than forty nine years," Jack muttered. "Don't those extra years count for something?"

"No." The angel smiled again, seeming unbothered by the accusation in Jack's tone.

His hands curled into fists and he tried to calm his temper. He should have learned how to keep it under control by now. Maybe he'd figure that trick out in another decade or two. "Assignments. Does that mean I finally get out of this place?"

"No. You'll be assigned students in need of help. Only your assignment can see or interact with you. Everything else will remain as it has always done."

There went plans of getting a bottle of whiskey. Jack glared at the angel, but the effort seemed to go unnoticed. "So who do I help?"

The angel gestured across the school grounds to the gaggle of girls who'd walked past him earlier. He indicated the girl in the middle of the group. "Your first assignment."

"Her!" He had to spend time with her while he was sober?

"Is there a problem? Would you rather spend an eternity in hell?"

"It feels like I already have."

"This is a holiday in comparison."

Jack glanced towards the girl again, wincing when one of her friends squealed at a teeth grinding pitch. "Fine. What have I got to do for her?"

"If I have to hold your hand I might as well do the job myself."

"Great. An angel with an attitude."

The smile could only be described as angelic. The answer was anything but. "You have your own sweet personality to thank for that."

Jack growled. "Haven't you got anything helpful to say?"

"Yes. Play by the rules."

"I was thinking of something," he used his hand to fill in the temporary blank. "You know… helpful."

"Oh, you want helpful." The angelic smile remained in place. "In that case, her name is Lucy." The angel vanished.

Jack swore. "Great. And that was so very helpful."

He stared after the group of girls. And he had to deal with them sober as a saint. He grunted. Or an angel. How lucky was he? He rolled his eyes heavenward. "Torture cannot be considered ethical, moral or in the least bit angelic." There was no reply to his words. He was used to that. He'd had more than forty-nine years of being ignored.

His gaze roamed over Lucy who seemed to be parting from the annoying crowd she hung with. The chick might be stacked but unless she came with a volume dial he wasn't going to survive a week with her. He sighed as he strode after her. Now he just had to find a moment when she wasn't surrounded by the ear bleeding horde, she regularly hung with, before he approached her. Letting her talk to him when others were around might make her appear insane. He didn't need anything else to atone for.

Chapter Four

Lucy

Lucy could see her front gate ahead and walked faster. Would there be another one? She didn't know, but she'd find out soon enough. She had been so tempted to leave school early and see who it was, but she had no clue when they visited her house. Reaching the front gate, she paused, her hand resting on the unpainted, weathered timber. What if they'd stopped? This was the start of the third week. Surely they wouldn't keep it up forever. There was only one way to find out.

Forcing herself to open the gate she took several hesitant steps forward, letting the gate close behind her. She remained standing just inside the gate, trying to see if there was anything on the small patio. It was too shadowy. She forced herself to stride to the front door. Her heart skipped a beat as she stepped onto the concrete of the patio. It was lying against the wall, to the side of the door. A white rose, barely formed. Some people might even have called it a rosebud. She glanced around. Seeing no one was about, she picked up the rose. Again she looked around. Other than the occasional car, the street was empty. Her eyes rested on the houses of some of her neighbours. They were either old people or ones with young kids so she was probably wasting her time checking if someone was watching her from the corner of a window.

She held the rose to her nose and breathed deeply. It was a light scent, just a hint of muskiness. She desperately wanted to know who was leaving them for her. If they were hanging around watching her pick them up like some of her friends thought, then she couldn't see them. They were too well hidden. Her gaze was drawn to a shady tree further up the street, surrounded by shrubs. Nothing. She couldn't see a single person.

She looked at the small white card attached with a white ribbon. Only her name, nothing else. The mystery was killing her. Did she know him? How was she going to find out who it was? After another look up and down the deserted street, she unlocked the front door and headed inside.

In her bedroom, Lucy ditched her schoolbag on the floor and added the latest rosebud to the vase sitting on her desk. There were eleven in various stages of health. One for each week day. They never arrived on the weekend so it had to be someone who knew her and knew there'd be someone at home to see them leave the rose. She reached out and rubbed a waxy petal between her fingers, unable to prevent a smile from forming. As frustrated as she was, she was also relieved.

Her secret admirer looked like he wasn't going to stop leaving her roses any time soon. Still staring at the vase of roses, Lucy tried to convince herself she should start her homework. What she would have preferred to do was find out who was sending her flowers. Maybe she could stake out a local florist. No, that'd be a waste of time since she couldn't be there constantly and she wouldn't know when to expect him. Or even which florist he used. She had no idea how to figure out who was leaving them. He didn't leave a single clue.

Her phone beeped, dragging her attention away from the roses. It was Jasmine. She'd told her friend she hadn't expected roses this week too. That she was half certain there wasn't going to be one waiting for her. Surely he wasn't going to keep sending them forever and never tell her who he was. She read the message. *Well?*

Her smile became a grin and she typed in the answer Jasmine had probably been waiting to hear. *Yes.* She was surprised Jasmine had waited this long to ask.

I wish I had a secret admirer. So unfair.

Tell Kurt to buy you roses.

He probably doesn't even know what they are.

Jasmine's words made her chuckle. *Yeah, probably give you a football instead.*

lol.

I have to start my homework. See you tomorrow at school.

Don't remind me. I've got too much of my own to do. Bye.

Placing her phone on her desk next to the vase, Lucy rummaged in her schoolbag until she had the homework she needed. After pushing her laptop towards the back of the desk she sat down, staring at the roses for several more minutes before she could bring herself to start. She was nowhere near finished when her sister, Leeah, burst into her room.

She could never look at her sister without thinking of the annoying phrase her father always used. They were not two peas in a pod. That always made her think of something fat and round. And she wasn't. Neither of them were. They had curves, but who wanted to look like a stick figure?

"Stop bursting into my room." She met Leeah's eyes, the exact same colour blue as her own.

"I need a favour." Leeah moved to look in the mirror hanging on the wall, finger combing and rearranging her short chestnut coloured hair.

She had the same colour hair as her sister, except hers was a little past her shoulders and had a slight wave to it. But just because Leeah was almost her look alike, that didn't mean she could enter her room whenever she felt like it. "Knock. How many times do I have to tell you?" She winced when she heard herself sounding like her mother.

Leeah finished rearranging her hair and turned to face her. "I don't have time for that. Justin sent me a text. He's on the way."

"No."

"I haven't asked anything yet."

She shook her head. "I already know what you're going to ask. And it's no." This time she'd be firm. It wasn't like her sister could make her do anything she didn't want to do.

"Aw come on, Lucy. We barely get any time together. Between uni, work and his brother we almost have no time alone. An hour tops. Well, maybe a bit more."

"We have nothing in common. I spend every minute trying to think of something to say to Dylan." There was nothing Leeah could say to convince her. Absolutely nothing. She didn't owe her a single favour.

"You both go to school. Talk about that."

"Different schools."

"So? They're all the same."

"No."

"I'll let you wear that dress of mine you love, next time you ask."

Lucy sighed. She'd asked Leeah a million times and had never been allowed to borrow it. Had never really expected her to say yes. The dress was perfect. But Dylan? He was the most awkward, boring person ever. She really wanted to borrow that dress. Sometimes her sister knew her too well. "The next two times I ask."

Leeah hesitated. "Done. If you don't take good care of it, you're dead."

"Sure. Then you'd have no one to keep Dylan busy while you drag Justin off to your room. With the door shut." She couldn't help a smile at the flicker of unease in Leeah's eyes. Not that she'd say anything, but she didn't want her sister thinking she could always talk her into whatever she wanted.

"You wouldn't tell Mum because I'd have just as much to tell her about you."

Lucy shrugged and rose from her desk, taking one last look at the vase. "When are they here?"

Leeah checked the time on her phone, sliding it back into her bra, the lace edge showing at the neck of her fitted black shirt, glittery stars scattered across the front of it. "Five minutes. I need to fix my make up." She dashed from the room as quickly as she'd entered it.

Lucy stared at her open door, reluctantly walking over to it to look down the hallway towards her sister's room. She hoped Justin and Dylan didn't stay long. She had homework to finish. Holding back a sigh, she slowly walked to the lounge room. Her eyes were drawn to the double seater lounge chair. There was no way she was going to make the same mistake as last time. She strode towards the single seater. Having to talk with Dylan was bad enough. She wasn't about to sit beside him too. Drumming her fingers on the arm of the cushioned armrest, Lucy tried to think of something she could say to Dylan. Talking about school was lame.

She still hadn't thought of anything by the time

she heard Justin's car coming down their street, the hole in the exhaust warning he was nearby. She didn't move towards the front door until the sound stopped.

The last thing she wanted to do was spend any time with Dylan. She pictured her sister's dress, trying to see herself in it. The image faltered as she opened the front door and saw Justin and Dylan headed towards her, Dylan several steps behind his brother.

There were some similarities between them. Both had sandy brown hair and blue eyes, but Dylan's hair always seemed greasy. They were both narrow framed, but where Justin was wiry, Dylan appeared gangly.

At the sound of footsteps behind her, Lucy turned to see her sister, a grin in place, coming towards her. "Justin." The word was an enthusiastic cry.

Lucy stepped out of the way, knowing from experience that her sister was about to launch herself at him. She waited until their kiss ended and Leeah dragged Justin back the way she'd come before she reluctantly looked at Dylan. "Hi."

He mumbled something that could have been 'hi' as he stared at the ground.

She looked past him at the front gate they'd left open, wondering if it was too late to escape. Probably. "You coming in?"

A quick nod, an even quicker glance at Lucy and Dylan hurried inside, stopping by the double seater.

Lucy was tempted to say, 'no way'. Instead she crossed to the armchair she'd sat in while she'd waited. Dylan continued to stand and Lucy bit back the impatient words that nearly spilled. "You going to sit?" She gestured towards the lounge chair he stood near.

With a jerky nod, he almost collapsed into the seat.

Why on earth did he have to come with his brother? Surely he found this as uncomfortable as she did. "Uhmm, how was school today?"

He gave another jerky nod, this one followed by a slight shrug. "Okay." His voice broke on the word.

They sat in silence for several minutes, Dylan's heel tapping up and down, only the toe of his sneakers touching the carpet. Lucy stared at it. So much for her sister's suggestion they talk about school. Obviously that wasn't going well. What was she meant to talk about now? She tried to remind herself of the dress. Was it worth this agony? Possibly. "Yeah, not much happens at school. It's a bit boring sometimes."

"Yeah."

She felt like shaking him and telling him to put some effort into the conversation. Reminding herself of the dress, she remained seated. Justin better not stay too long. An hour wasn't that long. Not usually. She looked around the lounge room trying to find inspiration. There was none. "Uhm, I was doing my maths homework. Nearly finished it. Just stuck on the last problem."

Dylan jumped to his feet in a rush. "Need some help?"

The words were all run together and it took Lucy a moment to figure out what he'd said. Did she really want him in her room? Surely letting him help her with her homework had to be better than sitting here struggling to find something to say. And she did need to get it done. She slowly nodded. "Okay." Rising to her feet, she led the way to her room, throwing glances over her shoulder to make sure he was still following.

Chapter Five

Lucy

Lucy paused in her bedroom doorway. A quick look showed everything was tidy enough and there was nothing embarrassing lying around. She stepped into the room and Dylan followed. The way his eyes searched her room made her feel uncomfortable. Striding towards her desk, she said, "It's over here. My homework."

Dylan followed her. "That's a lot of flowers. Who gave them to you?"

With her hand on the back of the desk chair, Lucy faced him. Finally, a conversation. One she hadn't started. "I don't know. They're on the doorstep every afternoon when I get home from school."

"How do you know they're not for Leeah?"

Lucy smiled. She'd thought the same thing the first

time she'd seen one. "Because they're addressed to me." It was still hard to believe. She reached for one of the cards on her desk and held it out to him. "See."

Dylan took the card, staring down at it. "Odd."

"What is?"

"Only your name, not theirs."

Her smile faded and she snatched the card back. "It's sweet. Romantic."

Dylan shrugged. "Why them?" He gestured towards the roses.

"I don't know, but they're pretty." Maybe she shouldn't have bothered trying to get him to talk. She fought the urge to tell him to shut up. Dress, think of the dress, she reminded herself.

"Maybe they mean something."

"White roses?"

Dylan nodded, his greasy hair flopping into his eyes. He brushed it out of the way.

"Possibly." Why hadn't she ever thought to look it up? Maybe there was a clue in the meaning.

Dylan pushed past her, leaning over her schoolwork to turn on the laptop. "I'll help."

Her hands started to curl into fists and she placed the card on the desk before she crushed it. "I can do it."

"Won't take me long." Dylan continued to lean

forward as he waited for the laptop to finish booting up.

Her lips tightened and she glared at him. Who did he think he was? Taking over her room like that. It was her laptop, not his. Next time her sister expected her to keep Dylan entertained she'd take a book and read while she sat in the lounge room with him. Better yet, there wasn't going to be a next time. She was beginning to think no dress, even a perfect one, was worth putting up with this.

Dylan pulled up a browser and his fingers flew across the keys. "Here." He tapped the screen with a finger, leaving a smudge behind.

Her eyes skimmed through the words on the page. "They're for brides and funerals. That doesn't sound good at all."

"You skipped most of the page. Look." His finger jabbed the screen again. "Purity, innocence, reverence, secrets."

"But they're still for brides and dead people. I'm not planning to be either for a very long time." It looked like searching out the meaning was a stupid idea. Whoever it was had probably chosen them because they looked nice.

Dylan turned to glare up at her. "You're focusing on the wrong part." He turned back to the screen, pulling up a different page. "Look at this one. They're the first rose. The ones all others came from. So they're important."

"It says it's a myth."

He pulled up another page. "He's saying he's worthy of you."

"That page also says they're too young for love."

"What about this one?" Dylan opened up one of the other links from his search. "White roses are the traditional rose for true love."

"But they aren't anymore. It says red roses now symbolise true love." This was a waste of time. There were no clues in the meaning of white roses.

Dylan glared at her. "It's obvious you're paying attention to the wrong information. You're the one who said it was sweet and romantic. So you need to look at the sweet and romantic parts. If it's sweet and romantic, obviously he wouldn't be thinking of dead people."

Her eyes were drawn to the time in the corner of the screen. How much longer until Justin left and took his brother with him? It better not be more than an hour. She managed not to sigh heavily, dredging up an insincere smile instead. She should change the topic before she said something she might regret. "I'm sure you're right. Now about my homework." She gestured towards the book still open on the desk that Dylan was leaning all over to be able to reach her laptop.

"Okay, but can we open the window some more? It's hot in here."

"No. The curtain knocks things off my desk if it's completely open. I'll turn the fan on." Once the fan was on, she was relieved Dylan forgot about the subject of the roses and helped with her homework. The time continued to creep by, but eventually Justin stood in the open doorway and said it was time to go. Nearly an hour and a half. Leeah was cutting it fine. Their parents would be home soon and she risked getting in trouble for having friends over on a week day. Leeah had argued for weeks that she should be allowed to have friends visit whenever she wanted, now she was at university. They hadn't agreed.

Lucy trailed behind the three of them to the front door, well behind Dylan who kept glancing back at her. As soon as Justin had driven off, Lucy turned to her sister. "That was the last time. No matter what you offer, the answer is no."

Leeah grinned. "Sure." She hurried away, laughing.

"I'm serious," she called after her sister as she closed and locked the front door before heading to her room. She was completely serious. There was no way she could go through that trauma again. She stopped by her desk and reached out to rub one of the waxy petals between her thumb and finger. True love. If that was the case, she hoped he didn't take too much longer to let her know who he was. She was getting sick of waiting.

She took a couple of tissues from the box sitting on her desk and cleaned the fingerprints off the screen of her laptop. Letting Dylan in her room hadn't been a good idea.

Chapter Six

Lucy

Lucy jumped the fence to cut through the treed section of the school rather than walk the long way round to the front gate. She'd nearly passed the groundsman's shed when a boy stepped out of the shadowy doorway. Her heart lurched, wavering between fear and excitement. This part of the school grounds was currently empty, but he didn't look dangerous. He actually made her think of old movies. Ones with people like James Dean, Elvis Presley or Audrey Hepburn. Maybe he was the one giving her roses.

"Lucy, I'm Jack Richards."

She nodded, not sure what she should say. 'How do you know my name' seemed a little too abrupt to ask, even though she wanted to know the answer. Asking him if he was the one leaving her roses probably wasn't good manners either.

Jack ran his fingers through his dark hair. "A pity the blasted bird wasn't more helpful. Look, apparently I need to help you."

That was the last comment she'd expected. Maybe he wasn't the one giving her roses after all. "With what?"

"I wish I knew. So, what do you need help with?"

She took a step backwards. It was possible he wasn't as harmless as he looked. Who dressed like they were out of some old movie from the fifties or sixties, right down to the leather jacket? "I have no idea what you're talking about." She glanced over her shoulder in the direction she needed to go. "Uhm, well… it was nice meeting you, Jack." She took another step away from him, wishing the area wasn't so deserted.

"I wasn't told what you need help with, just that you need it. So if you tell me how I can help, I can get it over and done with. The last thing I want is to be stuck here any longer than I have to."

"Yeah, okay, I'll think about that and get back to you." She slowly backed away, not wanting to make any sudden moves before she had a chance to put more space between them.

Jack chuckled, matching her step for step. "I

recognise that tone of voice. I've used it plenty of times myself. All I want to know is what you need help with. Then I'll get out of your life and you'll never have to see me again." He grinned. "Let's just say I'll be completely invisible to you."

She thought of the roses. Maybe that'd be enough to get him off her back. Anything was worth a try. "Someone's been leaving white rosebuds on my doorstep every weekday. I've been trying to figure out who it is."

Jack shook his head. "I doubt that'd be the problem. It's not important enough."

"It's important to me." She stopped retreating, relieved when Jack stopped walking towards her.

"It just–" He broke off, looking past her. "One of your friends is headed this way. So I suggest you stop talking to me and pretend I don't exist. Unless of course you want to look like a crazy person."

She turned to see Jasmine walking towards her, her lips curving into a smile when she caught her eye. About to ask Jack what he meant, he hurried past her and walked through her friend. Her mouth dropped open and she stared after Jack as he glanced behind, and with a wink, waved before he continued to walk away.

"Lucy?" Jasmine waved a hand back and forth in front of her face. "Are you okay?"

"I don't know." She continued to stare in the direction Jack had taken, no longer able to see him through the trees. What had just happened?

"Are you sick? Did something happen?"

She opened her mouth to ask Jasmine if she'd seen anybody, but closed it instead. How could she have seen Jack? If Jasmine had watched someone walk straight through her she'd probably be hysterical right this minute. Or would Jasmine be? She wasn't. Maybe she should ask her. She looked past Jasmine again trying to figure out what to do. "No, nothing happened. I'm okay." Hopefully. They were only a couple of months into the school year so she couldn't blame it on the pressure.

"Are you sure? What were you doing here anyway? I was expecting you ages ago. When I came looking for you, you were just standing there."

Going insane, apparently. "Thinking."

"About?"

Once more she looked in the direction Jack had taken. He was nowhere to be seen. "Uhm, roses." She felt dazed, like the world no longer made any sense.

Jasmine linked her arm through Lucy's. "It's so exciting. Are you sure you have no idea who it is."

"Not a single clue." She walked beside Jasmine, letting her friend's chatter wash over her as her eyes scanned the area. Who was Jack? And how on earth had he walked through Jasmine?

"Are you listening to me?" Jasmine shook her arm.

"Yeah."

"Well?"

She had no idea what Jasmine had asked her. All she could do was shrug.

"You don't think you're lucky? I wish I had a secret admirer."

She pieced together what Jasmine must have asked. "It's not that, I just wish I knew who it was."

"I bet he tells you eventually. I mean, he'll have to. It's not like you'll be able to guess. He hasn't left a single clue to help you figure it out."

"I know. I'm actually starting to think I don't know him. None of the guys we know are the slightest bit romantic." She glanced around the area once more. That wasn't the only thing she didn't have a clue about. Did Jack exist or was her mind playing tricks on her? As far as she knew all her family were completely normal, no history of insanity at all. But maybe that was something her parents wouldn't want to tell anyone, not even their daughters. For all she knew there was a great aunt locked away somewhere, completely insane.

"Are you sure no one has dropped any clues? Said anything? Done something to give you an idea?"

"Nothing. Not one single thing." Seeing a boy with mousy brown hair that she'd caught staring at her during lunch last week, she changed direction to avoid walking near him. He made her uncomfortable and she hadn't been amused when Jasmine had teased her that he might be the one sending her roses. He better not be. "I wish whoever it was would hurry up and tell me."

Jasmine glanced around. "It could be absolutely anyone." She giggled, nodding towards the boy Lucy was trying to avoid. "Even him."

"You're not funny, you know."

"I asked around and found out his name is Cole."

"What did you do that for? Now he'll think I'm interested in him." She glanced in Cole's direction and found him staring at her. Normally it didn't bother her if someone looked at her or even stared at her, but there was something about his eyes. They made her feel like he could see inside her and learn all her secrets. Not that she had many.

"He won't think that. It's not like I even mentioned your name."

Lucy was almost relieved when the rest of her friends joined them and took Jasmine's focus off her. She couldn't resist having one more look for Jack, deliberately not looking in Cole's direction. What was Jack? The word 'ghost' popped into her mind and she quickly discarded it. No way. Absolutely not possible at all.

When the bell finally rang, she said goodbye to her friends and hurried towards her classroom. Yet again she looked around for Jack, turning back in time to see someone loom up in front of her.

The boy sidestepped, laughing, putting out a hand to steady her. "Is there a fire I don't know about?"

The warmth of his hand soaked into her shoulder. He certainly wasn't a ghost. Again she thought of Jack. "Uhm, no. Sorry." Her eyes were drawn to the ground to stare at her shoes.

"Don't be. You can run into me any time." His hand dropped to his side.

She darted a glance in his direction to find he was still grinning. "Uhm." Her mind went blank and she felt a moment of sympathy for Dylan.

"So where have you been all my life?"

She laughed, a little nervously, a good touch of disbelief. "That has to be the worst line ever." She met his blue eyes, blond hair nearly falling into them. He had to be about ten centimetres taller than her so she was forced to tilt her head to meet them.

"Yeah, but it got you to talk to me, didn't it? You were about to keep running from your fire."

"I was running to class. Now I'm probably going to be late." Not that she was really as annoyed as she sounded. She'd much rather stand here talking.

The boy shrugged. "I doubt you're missing anything important." He held out his hand. "I'm Tanner."

She took it. "Lucy."

"Want to do something this weekend?"

She could barely believe she'd heard right. Things like this didn't happen to her. Random guys did not ask her out. The most unusual thing that had ever happened to her was the rosebuds on her doorstep. With the way things had been going lately it'd probably turn out that Cole was the one giving them to her. "Like what?"

"A movie?"

"Uhm, possibly."

"Excellent." He pulled out his phone. "What's your number?"

She rattled it off and took out her phone to put his number in. "Why?" She almost groaned when she heard herself ask. Did it really matter?

"Why what?"

It was too late now. She'd already started to ask. "Why did you ask me to go to the movies?"

He grinned. "Because you're as pretty as a flower." He shrugged. "Yeah, I know, super shallow of me, but since we've just met, what else can I go on?"

"A flower?" Was this it? Was this the clue she'd been waiting for? Her heart gave a lurch and she tried to remain calm.

"Yep."

Surely it couldn't be this easy. And he'd said flower, not rose. "Some flowers are ugly."

He laughed. "A rose. Does that sound better?"

"A white rose?" She almost held her breath as she waited for his answer.

"Sure. A white rose sounds good to me." He glanced over his shoulder at the sound of footsteps. "I'll call you later." He grinned again. "To think I was annoyed about moving here a few weeks ago."

"You're only new to this area?"

"Yep."

"When did you move here?" Lucy stared at him when he mentioned the date. Three days before she'd received her first rose. Was he her secret admirer? Maybe Dylan was right about her secret admirer eventually letting her know who he was. And maybe he just had. She smiled. "I'll talk to you later." Hurrying past him she glanced back to find he watched her. When he grinned, her own smile widened before she continued towards her classroom, not in the least bit worried about getting in trouble.

Her grin faded when she remembered Jack. Who was he and why hadn't Jasmine seen him? Was she going crazy? She had no idea and there was probably only one way to find out for certain. Return to the place she'd met him. She wasn't sure that was the best idea, but what else could she do? A feeling of dread washed over her. Maybe it'd be better to forget all about him. But she couldn't. The image of him walking through Jasmine kept playing over and over in her mind.

Chapter Seven

Lucy

The first chance Lucy had to return to the groundsman's shed was after school. As much as she wanted to hurry home and see if there was another rose waiting for her, she needed to find out if Jack existed. If she did find him, she didn't know what she'd do. Run screaming? Isn't that what you did for ghosts?

Reaching the shed, she stood in front of it and stared at the closed door. Now what was she meant to do? She looked around the area. In the distance she could hear the sound of students as they left for the day. Nearby there was no one. She was all alone, in a cluster of trees, standing in front of a locked building. What was she thinking? There was no one here. She should go home. Taking a single step back, she hesitated. She had no idea where else to look for him. Whoever he was, or whatever he was, he was gone.

She sighed, one of relief, as she turned away. It looked like she could forget all about him. "Jack." The word was little louder than her sigh had been. She opened her mouth to say 'goodbye and good riddance'.

"Did you figure it out?"

She almost screamed when she heard Jack speak. Spinning to face him, her hand pressed against her heart, she demanded, "Where did you come from?"

"I guess you don't pay much attention in class if you need to ask that question. I've noticed you've had some fairly detailed classes on the birds and bees. Not like in my day."

She ignored his grin, tempted to shake her head and possibly even roll her eyes. "Who are you?"

"I've already told you. Jack."

"And who exactly is Jack?"

"Look, that isn't important. Tell me what you need help with so I can get it over and done with."

Remembering how he'd walked through Jasmine earlier, she reluctantly took a couple of steps forward and reached out to touch his shoulder. She drew her hand back. He was as solid and warm as her. "How did you do that earlier?"

"Do what?"

"Don't be so annoying. You know exactly what I mean. How did you walk through Jasmine?"

He held out his hand.

She stared at it, wanting to back away.

"Go on, take it." He nodded towards his hand.

It took her a moment before she could bring herself to reach out and grasp his hand. It was solid and warm, just like his shoulder had been. His fingers wrapped around hers. When she tried to tug away from him, his grip tightened. She started to say something, but all of a sudden, he was no longer solid and his hand passed through hers. Then he was reaching for her hand as she tried to pull it towards herself. He was quicker than her and held her hand in both of his, once again solid. "How did you do that?" Her words were little more than a breath of air. If he hadn't been holding her hand so tight she probably would have been over the fence and halfway home by now. As it was, she didn't know why she wasn't screaming. This couldn't be happening to her.

"I guess some people would call me a ghost."

"Some?" Her voice was higher pitched than usual.

Maybe that scream would happen after all. "What do you call yourself?"

He laughed, a humourless mocking sound. "Damned."

She had no idea what to say to that. This time when she tugged on her hand, he let go. She tried desperately to think of something to say, wondering why she wasn't running. But he'd sounded so lost when he'd said the word damned. Maybe he was the one who actually needed help, not her. "Who said I needed help?"

He laughed again, the same sound as before. "An angel."

"As in wings, robes and a harp?" She didn't even bother trying to keep the disbelief from her voice. A ghost was hard enough to comprehend, but an angel too? No, absolutely not. It wasn't possible.

"He's certainly got the wings, but I've never seen any harp. I'd probably be tempted to shove it down his throat if I did."

He sounded serious and once again she wasn't certain what to say. "Uhm, well I don't think he knew what he was talking about. Maybe he got me mixed up with someone else."

"I doubt it. I'm sure he's far too perfect to make a mistake like that."

She couldn't miss hearing the bitterness in his voice. "I can't think of any problem other than not knowing who's leaving me flowers. But I may have figured that out."

"I've already said it can't be that."

"I don't have any other problems." There had to be a way to convince him to get out of her life. She didn't need his help. All he was doing was making her doubt her own sanity.

"You must do."

Lucy started to speak, but stopped when her phone rang. Drawing it out, she smiled when she saw the display read 'Tanner'. It was odd that he rang not long after she'd been thinking about him. She turned away from Jack before she answered. "Hi." He had very good timing.

"I didn't ask you where you live. It'll be a bit hard to pick you up and take you to the movies this weekend if I don't know that."

"Only a couple of streets away. Close enough that I walk home from school."

"Really? I suppose you've already left."

"Not exactly. Nearly though." She glared at Jack who stepped into her view.

"Do you want a lift?"

"Uhm, sure." She ignored Jack, who was shaking his head and told Tanner where to meet her.

Chapter Eight

Lucy

Jack didn't even wait for her to finish hanging up before he demanded, "What do you think you're doing? You don't even know him. I saw you meet him earlier today. Don't they teach stranger danger anymore?"

"If you saw me meet him then you know he goes to this school. I have to go. Tanner will be waiting for me in a minute."

"When are you going to tell me what you need help with?"

"I've already told you. I'm fine. I don't need help with anything. Find someone else to help." She headed towards the fence.

Jack walked beside her. "It doesn't work like that.

It's you I have to help. Call for me the moment you know how I can help."

Reaching the fence, she paused to look at Jack before she jumped over it. Maybe if she humoured him he'd quit annoying her. "Have you got a number I can ring you on?"

Jack laughed. "I'm a ghost. I don't need a phone. You know my name. Call me."

She watched him walk away, turning before he'd completely disappeared amongst the trees. A car pulled up and the window was wound down. Seeing Tanner in the driver's seat, she headed for the car, returning his grin.

It didn't take them long to reach her place and she almost groaned at the sight of Justin's car parked out the front. More than likely Dylan would be with him. At the moment she wished she didn't live so close to school. The drive had been far too short. "Thanks for the lift." She opened the door.

"Aren't you going to invite me in?"

There was no way she wanted to risk him thinking Dylan was her friend. Smiling, she shook her head. "No, I'm not allowed friends over after school. Only on the weekend." If Justin's car hadn't been parked out the front, she would have ignored the rule and invited him in.

"So you'll invite me in on the weekend?"

She clambered out of the car, her smile still in place. "Possibly." More than likely. Closing the door, she returned Tanner's wave before she opened the gate and strode towards the house. Seeing the rosebud near the door, she looked over her shoulder to where Tanner sat in his car. Was he leaving the roses for her? She waved again. He returned her wave before he drove off. Picking up the rose she headed inside, freezing when she saw Dylan waiting for her.

"Who was that?"

She guessed her sister wouldn't appreciate it if she told him 'none of your business'. Why didn't Justin tell him to find something else to do rather than letting him tag along? "A friend."

"A close friend?"

She shrugged. Did he have to keep questioning her? It really wasn't any of his business. "I need to…" She glanced around trying to think of an excuse, her eyes falling on the rosebud she held. "Put this in my vase." She hurried away before he could say anything else. The moment she was in her room she locked the door.

She crossed the room to her desk and started to put the rose in the vase. Instead, she held it to her nose, breathing in deep as she closed her eyes. Opening them, she stared at the white petals, wondering when she'd find out who was giving them to her. It was taking too long. She put the rose in the vase with the rest of them and dropped onto her bed to stare at the ceiling. There was no way she was leaving her room until Dylan left. She certainly didn't lack things to do. There was her homework for starters. Or maybe she could do a search on the meaning of white roses. Dylan might have been looking at all the wrong sites.

There was a soft tap on her door. She turned her head to stare at it. There was a slightly louder knock. Surely it wasn't Dylan. Rising to her feet, she crossed the room, listening to one more knock before she opened it. Dylan stood in front of her. She nearly swore.

"Do you need help with your homework again?"

She started to say no, then shrugged. He had helped her with what she'd been stuck on yesterday. Once he'd finished taking over her laptop. Which shouldn't be a problem today since there was no need to turn it on. "I haven't looked at it yet."

"I can help you if you need some."

"Uhm…" She could only think to repeat her previous comment. Obviously it hadn't made any difference saying it the first time so she doubted saying it a second time would help. Before she could come up with anything else to say, Leeah's bedroom door opened and her and Justin stepped into the hall.

"Who dropped you home? Is that your new boyfriend?" Leeah said the last word in a singsong voice.

Lucy rolled her eyes. "You're such a child sometimes." A pity her sister's room faced the front yard. She was probably going to tease her about Tanner for weeks. Payback sucked.

"He's your boyfriend?" Dylan asked.

Lucy didn't have a chance to answer. Justin spoke. "We've got to go. Mum rang. Someone left the kitchen in a mess." He looked pointedly at Dylan.

"It was your turn to clean up."

Lucy watched as the two of them walked away arguing. Leeah went with them. Relieved, Lucy stepped back into her bedroom and closed the door, leaning against it. She wasn't about to stand around and wait for Leeah to return and question her about Tanner. She barely knew the boy. Her eyes were drawn to the vase filled with roses. There was now a dozen. She smiled. Maybe he was her secret admirer, maybe he wasn't. She couldn't resist crossing the room and lifting the latest one from the vase to gently brush her fingers across the petals. Hopefully she'd find out by the weekend. Holding it to her nose, she inhaled. Whoever it was, they certainly had good taste in roses.

Chapter Nine

Lucy

Lucy slowly looked at each of the boys sitting in front of her in the classroom. She really hoped none of them were her secret admirer. Why wasn't he letting her know? How many weeks was he going to leave her wondering? She looked at the students sitting to her left. There was only one boy. Nope, she didn't want it to be him either. He talked with his mouth full and sprayed all those near him with food. So it better not be him.

She also hoped it wasn't Cole. She'd caught him staring at her at lunch yesterday and for a moment she'd thought he was actually going to walk towards her. Then Tanner had joined her and Cole had glared at her before he'd turned away. Hopefully he hadn't learned that Jasmine had been asking about him for her.

"It's Thursday, how long do you need to figure out what I can help you with?"

Lucy barely managed not to scream when Jack stopped beside her desk, cutting off her view of the boy she stared at. She started to tell him to go away, then remembered only she could see him. Instead she wrote the words 'go away' at the top of the page on her schoolbook.

"Do you think I'm having a blast waiting for you to figure it out? Why do you have to be surrounded by those chicks all the time? And why have all of you got to spend half your time giggling?"

She underlined the words she'd written. Then drew a second line when he continued to stand there, tapping her pen lightly on the page beside the word. She considered asking to be excused to use the bathroom. It was frustrating not being able to argue with him. She didn't need his help. He was annoying her for no reason.

"Come and see me at lunch or I'll join you for the rest of your afternoon classes."

She watched him stride across the room, walking through the wall. A glance around showed she was still the only one who could see him. She doubted the rest of her classmates would be sitting there calmly, some of them looking half asleep, if they'd seen Jack walk through a wall. Great. Just great. That made two crappy days in a row. Yesterday Dylan had been at her house again, full of questions about who was giving her a lift home. Today Jack was hassling her. She really hoped Dylan wasn't at her place this afternoon. Especially if Tanner dropped her home again.

Yesterday afternoon she'd been tempted to ask Tanner if he'd been the one leaving her the rosebuds, but she hadn't been able to bring herself to raise the question. Not even when he'd sat with her at lunch yesterday. He'd asked her this morning if she'd join him for lunch today and she'd said yes. She couldn't be in two places at once. There was also no way she wanted to have Jack hassling her for the rest of the afternoon. She was likely to say something to him. Then everyone would think she was crazy and that she talked to people who didn't exist. That was all she needed.

When the bell finally rang for lunch, she almost ran to the groundsman's shed. Jack was waiting for her. "I thought you said you're meant to help, not hassle me. What you're doing is the complete opposite of help." She'd thought if she didn't bother calling him he'd leave her alone.

"Then tell me how I can help." His voice was filled with exasperation.

He had no reason to be exasperated. She was the only one who should be. There had to be some way to convince him to stop bothering her. "I don't need help with anything. I'm fine." She started to turn away.

"Look, that blasted bird wouldn't have said you needed help if you didn't need any."

"I don't have time for this, Jack. I'm meant to be having lunch with Tanner."

"Maybe he's the problem. The angel said you needed my help just before you met him."

"Oh no you don't. I'm not going to let you ruin things between me and Tanner." She shook her head, backing away. "I've already said I'd call you if I think of anything. Now quit bugging me." She spun away before he could say anything, hoping Tanner was still waiting for her. She was relieved to find him where they'd organised to meet. And when he didn't ask why she was late, she guessed it hadn't taken that long to talk to Jack.

She had no idea what Jack was meant to help with, but doubted it had anything to do with Tanner.

There was absolutely nothing wrong with him. The only problem she currently had was Jack. And not knowing who was leaving the roses. Although she was almost certain it was Tanner. There were too many coincidences for it not to be him. Pushing all her problems from her mind, she focused on what Tanner was saying, hoping she hadn't missed anything important. If she had, it was Jack's fault.

Lunch was over far too quickly and she reluctantly returned to class, once again agreeing to meet Tanner after school. The rest of her classes seemed to take an excessively long time to finish. When the final bell sounded, it was all she could do not to run out to where Tanner's car was parked. She grinned when she saw he was waiting for her, leaning against his bonnet. He must have run. There was no other way he could have arrived before her since his final classroom had been further away than hers.

Feeling like someone was watching her, she looked off to her left, half expecting Jack. Instead she saw Cole, his arms crossed as he leaned against the side of a building, shadows preventing her from seeing his expression. Her footsteps slowed and she felt like going over to him and demanding that he stop staring at her all the time, but she didn't want to encourage him. Forcing herself to ignore Cole, she turned her gaze to Tanner and continued to walk towards him.

He pushed away from the car as she reached him. "Do you need to go straight home?"

"I'm supposed to."

"So I can't convince you to have something to eat with me? It wouldn't take all afternoon. I was thinking fast food."

Her parents wouldn't be home until much later. It'd only be her sister at home. And Leeah more than owed her for all the times she'd covered for her. A smile slowly formed. "As long as I'm home by four." That should give her plenty of time to get enough homework done to make it look like she'd been there all afternoon.

Tanner grinned. "Let's go then."

She hopped in the car, her smile still in place as she sent her sister a text to let her know she'd be late. Maybe the day wouldn't be so bad after all. If she could only figure out how to stop Jack from hassling her then she wouldn't have a single problem in her life. She pushed him from her mind and turned to Tanner.

All through the drive and their meal they spoke about siblings, where Tanner had lived previously and school. When it grew closer to four and it was time to leave, Lucy wanted to protest. But she didn't. She needed to be home well before her parents if she didn't want to risk being grounded on the weekend. That was the last thing she wanted since she was really looking forward to going to the movies on Saturday. When they pulled up in front of her house, she reluctantly got out of Tanner's car. Eyeing Justin's car, she hoped he didn't have Dylan with him. Surely he could manage to visit without his brother. Hopefully her sister's relationship with Justin would be as short as the last two and she wouldn't have to put up with Dylan much longer.

Tanner got out of the car and joined her on the footpath. "I'll see you at school tomorrow." He hesitated. "Unless you want a lift in the morning?"

She wished she could say yes, but didn't think her parents would agree. She shook her head. "My sister drops me off on her way to uni each morning." She started to explain that her sister dropped her at the beginning of the street leading to school so she didn't have to go out of her way, but managed to stop the urge to babble nervously.

"If you change your mind, ring me." He stepped closer.

"Okay." She tilted her head to meet his blue eyes. They were a much darker blue than hers.

He took the last step separating them, one hand resting low on her back, the other at the nape of her neck. He stared down at her for several seconds, before his lips met hers.

Lucy wrapped her arms around him, her eyes closing as she returned his kiss. When it ended, she wanted to protest and drag him back to her. As much as she didn't want to, she needed to get inside and start her homework before her parents arrived home.

Tanner grinned at her. "You sure you don't need a lift in the morning?"

Lucy laughed softly. "Positive. I'll see you at school." She leaned forward and gave him one last kiss before she pulled away from him, running through the open gate to her front door. When she reached it, she looked back at him. He stood there watching her. Waving, he sauntered around to the driver's door, pausing to look over the roof of the car at her before he hopped in and drove off.

She almost didn't notice the rosebud on the patio near the wall. She had the door half open before she thought to check. Picking it up, she headed inside and nearly groaned when she found Dylan standing there staring at her. She had no idea what to say to him. All she wanted to do was escape to her room and do her homework. And probably reminisce about the kiss. Except she couldn't because Dylan was blocking her way. After discarding several comments and finally deciding to push past him, he spoke.

"I thought he wasn't your boyfriend. You said he was only a friend."

She shrugged. "Things change."

"So he's your boyfriend now?"

Not quite certain of the answer to that question, she shrugged again. "I need to go to my room."

Dylan remained in the way, staring at her.

"Uhm, can I get past?" When he didn't move straight away, she started to ask him again.

"Why?"

She frowned. Hadn't she already told him that? "I need to go to my room."

He shook his head. "No, why are you with him?"

"Uhm…" She was seriously tempted to say 'none of your business'. Surely Leeah would understand. Even she didn't put up with people questioning her. But she'd warned her numerous times to be nice to Dylan. That Justin was protective of his brother.

"Is it because he has a car?"

"What?" His comment didn't make the slightest bit of sense to her.

"Is he your boyfriend because he has a car?" When she didn't answer immediately, Dylan spoke again. "I had a girl tell me late last year that she never went out with any guy that didn't have a car."

She shook her head. "No. A car isn't important. There's always buses if I want to go somewhere that isn't in walking distance." She wondered if the girl had been trying to find a polite way to say no. "I like him." Very much. But that certainly wasn't any of his business.

Dylan stared at her a moment longer before he stepped to the side so she could walk past.

She hurried to her room, not even looking back to see if he still watched her. She'd rather not know. Closing her door, she locked it and put the rose in the vase before she dropped onto her bed. She should probably start her homework, but she'd much rather remember the kiss. She couldn't resist smiling. Even seeing Dylan as soon as she'd entered the house hadn't ruined the moment. She couldn't wait to go to the movies with Tanner Saturday night. Maybe by then she'd have worked up the courage to ask him if he was the one leaving roses for her. Although she doubted it. More than likely it'd take her a couple of weeks before she could convince herself to ask him.

Chapter Ten

Lucy

Jack cornered her the next morning when she walked past the groundsman's shed. Maybe she should take a different path in future, even if it would take her longer to get to her first class.

"I'm glad to see you survived the date."

It hadn't really been a date. They'd only grabbed a couple of burgers. "You were worried for no reason. Tanner's nice."

"You don't really know that."

"Yeah, I do. There's nothing wrong with him. He's nice. I don't need your help. I guess angels get things wrong sometimes. Unless you want to figure out who's leaving me rosebuds there's nothing you can help me with." If only she could figure out how to get him to accept that.

Jack shook his head. "There's got to be something."

"Why does there have to be something?"

Jack stared at her for a moment. "Because I'm meant to help you."

"Why? Are you some kind of guardian angel or something?" She had a feeling he was trying to avoid answering her.

Jack laughed, a humourless mocking one. "I'm as far from that as it's possible to get."

"Then why are you meant to help me?"

"Because I have to atone for every single sin I've ever committed. Even the little ones. It was that or hell. I've been assured I probably wouldn't like it."

"Hell?" She'd always thought it was about as real as angels. She struggled to recall everything she'd ever heard about it. "I guess you must have done something pretty bad to be headed there."

Once again he remained silent for a moment before he spoke. "Yeah. I killed my girlfriend and her new boyfriend."

She took a step back from him. "You… you did what?"

His lips twisted into a wry smile. "I had a gun." He paused, his eyes losing focus. "You know I can still hear the sound of it. I haven't forgotten one second of that day. It plays over and over in my mind like a broken record."

He looked so harmless. Surely he hadn't really killed two people. And one of them his girlfriend. "You're saying that so I won't have anything more to do with Tanner, aren't you?"

"No." He glanced past her. "Come on, before your blasted friend finds us." He grabbed her by the arm and tugged her inside the shed. "What does she think she is? Your shadow?"

She pulled away from him, remaining just inside the shed. "You tell me you've killed people and then you expect me to go into a dimly lit building with you. Are you crazy?"

"Anything is possible. I've spent decades with only myself to talk to, so I wouldn't be surprised if I was."

She momentarily closed her eyes. The conversation was a long way from where it had started. "I don't need your help, so please leave me alone."

Jack stared at her silently for nearly a minute. "I can't. I'm sorry, but I can't. I have to help you. I'm sick of being stuck here and helping you is the only way I can work towards getting out of this place."

She felt like growling in frustration. "Help someone else instead. I don't need any help. I'm fine.

There's absolutely nothing wrong with me or my life."

"I can't. He was very specific. You're the one I need to help."

She opened her mouth to speak, but the school bell rang. "I have to go." She took a step away from him, holding up a hand to halt him when he started to follow. "If I think of anything, I'll let you know."

"You know where to find me."

She nodded before turning and hurrying out of the shed, seeing Jasmine headed back towards the classrooms. Checking over her shoulder she saw Jack stood in the doorway. She couldn't help him. There wasn't a single problem in her life that needed dealing with. She ran after her friend. "Hey, Jasmine. Wait up."

Jasmine stopped, turning to face her. "Where were you?"

Reaching her friend's side, she linked arms with her. She ignored the question she couldn't answer without causing even more unanswerable questions. "You'll never guess what happened yesterday afternoon."

"Well, I guess from your expression it must have been good. So why didn't you ring or text me last night and tell me?"

"Because I wanted to tell you in person." That sounded much better than she hadn't wanted to share it with anyone. Not after all of Dylan's questions.

"Then hurry up or we'll be at our classroom and I won't get a chance to find out."

She briefly told Jasmine about going out for something to eat with Tanner yesterday afternoon, followed by the kiss. She winced at her friend's ear splitting squeal. When Jasmine started to ask a question, she shushed her. "He's behind you, headed this way." Luckily he wasn't close enough that he would have heard anything she'd said to Jasmine.

After a glance over her shoulder, Jasmine giggled. "Tell me later." With another giggle and a glance towards Tanner, she hurried off.

Tanner reached her side. "Meet me at lunch?"

"Yes."

He grinned, reaching for her hand and linking his fingers through hers. "I'll see you then." His fingers momentarily tightened on hers before he let go and hurried off.

She watched him walk away, grinning back at him when he glanced over his shoulder before disappearing round a corner. She headed into her own class, trying not to smile as she apologised for being late. Her teacher probably would have taken it the wrong way.

When lunch finally arrived, Lucy hurried towards where she usually met Tanner. She turned a corner and came face to face with Cole. It was too late to go in a different direction. His gaze cut through her as they walked past each other and she wondered what his problem was. He'd gone from staring to glaring at her in the space of a few days. Maybe he hadn't liked Jasmine asking about him. Other than that, she had no idea what she could have done wrong.

She checked over her shoulder to make sure he wasn't looking in her direction. He wasn't. Relieved, she continued towards where she was to meet Tanner. She really hoped Cole wasn't the one sending her flowers. Seeing Tanner, she grinned, picking up her pace.

Chapter Eleven

Lucy

Apart from lunch, which went far too fast, the rest of the day dragged until it was time to head home. When Tanner pulled up in front of her house, she wanted to suggest they go somewhere else instead. She didn't want to say goodbye yet.

Tanner leaned towards her, reaching for her. "I'll see you tomorrow night."

Before she had a chance to reply, his lips met hers. Then she didn't care about replying, only holding him close. Eventually she reluctantly pulled away from him, opening the car door. She remained in the seat, meeting his intense gaze. Finally, remembering his comment, she nodded. "I'll see you tomorrow night." She held his gaze a moment longer before she got out of the car, closing the door behind her. When she reached the front door she turned and waved to him as he drove off.

She continued to stare in the direction he'd taken, well after he'd disappeared. It was only then that she realised Justin's car wasn't parked out the front. She couldn't help grinning. An afternoon without having to put up with Dylan. That was certainly an event worth celebrating. At least she hoped so. For all she knew they'd come home in Leeah's car. She looked towards the closed doors of the double garage. If her sister was at home.

Before she opened the front door, she checked for a rosebud. Her good mood ended along with her smile. Heart racing, she bent down to pick up the rose, careful to touch only the stem. She stared at it. There were bright red splatters across the white petals. At first she thought it was blood. A closer look showed it was probably ink. Who would do something like this? Surely not her secret admirer. If Dylan had been visiting, she would have blamed it on him. Okay, so maybe he wouldn't have done it. Just because she found him annoying it didn't mean he'd do something like this. He'd even helped her try to find the meaning of white roses so she doubted it would have been him. But who would have done it? She thought of Cole who'd glared at her. It probably wouldn't be him either. She bet he didn't even know where she lived.

She looked up and down the street. No one was about. Now she had two questions to answer. Who was her secret admirer and who hated her? So much for telling Jack there was nothing he could help with. She stared at the bright red droplets. Hopefully he'd be able to help her find out who'd done that to her rose. Maybe that's why the angel had told him to help her. Although why an angel would tell him that she had no idea. Especially since she didn't believe in them.

Once in her room, she dropped the rose into the wastepaper bin, watching as streaks of red smeared across the crumpled paper that was in it. Her attention was drawn to her curtain when it flapped in the breeze.

"No!" She slammed her window shut, panic rushing through her as she pulled a handful of tissues from the box on the edge of the desk to mop up the water from her fallen vase. She righted the vase, but the roses remain scattered. She eyed the area around her laptop and breathed out heavily when she saw it was dry. Only the edge of her desk and the carpet had been wet. Luckily she never put much water in the vase. The sodden tissues were thrown in the bin, causing the red ink to smear further. For a moment she couldn't drag her eyes away from the spreading stains.

Why had her window been wide open? She never opened it completely. Her sister better not have been in her room or she'd make her life miserable. Striding to her sister's room, she banged on the door. There was no answer. Swinging it open, she saw the room was empty. Maybe Leeah had been home earlier and had gone already. She walked slowly back to her room as she took her phone from her pocket, ringing her sister's number.

As soon as Leeah answered, she demanded, "Were you home earlier?"

"No. Not that it's any of your business where I go. I don't whinge at you when you're late. Did I yesterday?"

"It's not that. Someone's been messing with my stuff." Reaching her room, she sat on the edge of her bed.

"As if. Why would I want to mess with your stuff?"

"My window was open."

"It was probably Mum. She's always complaining you should open your window and let more fresh air in."

"I suppose. When will you be home?"

"I don't know. Later. Much later. Before Mum and Dad get home."

"Okay." Once she hung up, she returned her phone to her pocket and slid off the bed. She slowly crossed the room to stare at the roses scattered across the corner of her desk, some of the petals having fallen on the floor. She probably should throw out the older ones. There was no point in keeping them.

Picking up the ones that were still fine, she returned them to the vase, throwing the rest in the bin. Gathering up the petals from the floor, she carefully put them in some crumpled paper so they didn't fall through the small love heart holes scattered randomly across the sides. She stared at the mess, deciding to take it outside to empty it in the wheelie bin. She'd barely stepped back inside the front door when her phone rang. Seeing it was her sister, she wondered what she'd forgotten to say. "Yeah?"

"Mum's ringing you. Tell her I'm at home. I'm not far away, all right?"

"Okay." Her sister hung up before she could ask her what was going on. Shrugging, she slid her phone back in her pocket and headed for her bedroom. She guessed she'd find out soon enough.

The phone didn't ring again until after she'd

returned her bin to its spot beside her desk. Checking the display, she saw it was her mother. "Yeah?"

"Do you remember that weekend for two I tried to win last month?"

"Yeah." Her word was hesitant as she tried to figure out why her mother would be bringing it up again. It didn't seem important enough for her to ring from work about it. "I remember. One of your friends won. Dad said he didn't know why you'd bothered since neither of you ever win anything."

"Yes, that's the one. Well my friend and her husband can't go. He broke his leg this afternoon and she's currently sitting up at the hospital with him. She offered the weekend away to your father and me."

"Okay." She wondered how he'd broken his leg, but guessed she'd hear all about it during dinner tonight. Probably more details than she really wanted to know.

"Does that okay mean you're happy for your sister to look after you for the weekend?"

She tried to keep the enthusiasm from her voice when all she wanted to do was jump up and down on the spot saying 'yes' over and over again. "Sure. As long as I still get to go to the movies tomorrow night like you agreed." She was pretty certain her voice sounded normal and didn't give away any of her excitement.

"Come straight home once the movie is finished."

"Okay."

"And I want you to pack our bags. We need to head straight from work. We won't have time to come home and pack before we leave. Not without being late. You're far more organised, when it comes to packing, than your sister. Leeah can drop the suitcase off to me at work. Are you sure you're happy to have your sister look after you this weekend? You won't fight with each other, will you?"

Lucy grinned. They were going this afternoon? Even better. "Sure. We'll be okay." It was an effort to keep her tone normal. She wanted to scream excitedly. There was no way she was heading straight home after the movie. No way at all and she doubted Leah would make her.

"You ring me if you have the slightest problem. No matter what time it is."

"We'll be fine, Mum." It took her nearly ten minutes to reassure her mother. While she continued to speak to her, she packed clothes for her parents, several times asking her mother which garment she preferred. By the time she got off the phone, the suitcase was packed and her sister had arrived.

Leeah took the suitcase. "I was planning to go to a party with Justin tonight."

Lucy shrugged. "It doesn't bother me. I don't care if you're here or not."

Leeah stared at her for a moment, a smile slowly forming. "You won't tell Mum and Dad if I stay at Justin's place tonight?"

"As long as I don't have to come straight home after the movie tomorrow night."

Leeah grinned. "Deal. I'll see you tomorrow." She hurried away before Lucy had a chance to say another word.

Chapter Twelve

Lucy

Hearing the front door close, Lucy finally let a squeal escape. She had the entire house to herself. Striding to the lounge room, she put on the stereo and turned the volume up. As the music filled the room, she spun around, her eyes closed, still grinning. It was the first time she'd ever had the house to herself overnight. Maybe she could ring Jasmine and invite her over.

She immediately discarded the idea. Jasmine's mother might say something to hers since they both knew each other.

Next she thought about calling Tanner, but then worried about what he might expect. She wandered through the house, peering into silent rooms, trying to decide what to do. Even turning the music up louder didn't help. In the end, she decided to do her homework and have dinner. After a phone call from her mother, to check she was okay, Lucy shook her head in disgust. She had the place to herself, no adults for the entire weekend, and she was sitting at home doing schoolwork.

Feeling beyond pathetic, she decided to go for a walk, leaving the patio light on when she locked the front door behind her. Having no idea where to go, her aimless wanderings ended up taking her towards school. Ahead she saw the fence she normally jumped over, Jack leaning against the top of it, looking in her direction. Stopping on the footpath, she stared at his figure that was mostly shadows, even with the streetlight on the other side of the road. She crossed the short distance between them, remaining outside the fence. "How did you know I was here? I didn't call you." At least she didn't think she had, but who knew how this worked.

Jack shrugged. "I've been able to find you ever since the angel said I needed to help you. I always know where you are. I'm guessing once I help you, that ability will disappear. Along with your ability to see me."

"What will happen to you then?"

"I'll help someone else. And keep helping people

until I've atoned for all I've done. Have you figured out what you need help with yet?"

She didn't know if she needed help with it, but at least it was something to tell him. Hopefully he'd be much happier with this problem than the first one she'd given him. "Someone tipped red ink all over my rosebud today. I thought it was blood at first."

"Who?"

"I don't know." She thought of the vase that had been knocked over. She doubted anyone would have been inside. There were no broken windows or anything.

"I can't leave the school grounds. I'm stuck here."

He could have told her that earlier. "Then how are you meant to help me?"

Jack started to speak then stopped to look past her. "A group of people are coming towards us. Hop over the fence and let's get away from here."

She glanced behind her and saw a group of kids on the road, headed her way. She pressed her hands against the top of the fence, vaulting over it to follow Jack to the groundsman's shed. When he walked through the locked door, she heard a click as it unlocked and swung open.

Taking out her phone, she used the screen like a

torch and, entering the room, closed the door behind her. "Nifty trick." She nodded towards the door.

"It doesn't always work." He walked further into the room. "Come on, this way."

She wound her way through tools and broken furniture, stacked boxes and cluttered shelves. Squeezing between a wall and an old wardrobe she found an empty place in a corner where Jack sat, leaning against the wall with one leg drawn up to rest his arm on.

"Why did you come here? Is something wrong? Did something else happen other than the ink on the rose?"

She shook her head, then shrugged, not quite sure what to tell him. "I don't know. My window was wide open, but that was probably my mum. She often opens it even though I've told her not to. I've thought about moving my room around so the curtain doesn't mess everything up on my desk, but then I'd be stuck with my bed under the window. Which would be worse. I'd have the sun waking me early every morning when the curtain moves in the breeze."

"Someone was in your room?"

She shook her head. "No, I guess not. I'm probably feeling jittery because the house is empty. I've never been there before on my own at night." She'd thought staying home alone would have been more fun.

"Where is everyone?"

By the time Lucy finished telling him about her parents going away for the weekend and her sister being at her boyfriend's as well as answered some of the other questions Jack had, it was nearly midnight. She stared at the time on her phone. "I should probably go." She didn't feel tired yet.

Jack rose to his feet and held out a hand to her. "Be careful walking home. Don't forget I can't leave the school grounds. Not for any reason."

Taking his hand, she let him tug her to her feet. She continued to hold his hand. "You don't feel like a ghost." His hand was warm in hers.

"What do I feel like?"

The light from the screen went out and the room plunged into darkness. "You feel alive." She wished she'd thought to turn her screen light back on before she'd spoken so she could see his expression. She did it now and met his dark eyes. "Why did you do it?" She started to clarify her question, when he spoke.

"I never meant to. If I could have undone it, I would have."

"Why? If you never meant to do it then what happened?"

There was a long pause before Jack answered. "Life." He drew his hand away from hers.

Her hand felt cold after his warmth. How could he feel so warm and alive if he was a ghost? It didn't seem possible. "What do you miss the most?"

Jack stared at her, his expression unfathomable. "Everything. Every single thing, but especially Rose." He stared at her a moment longer before he gestured towards the gap between the wardrobe and wall. "Weren't you going?"

She nodded and stared at Jack for nearly a minute before she squeezed through the gap. She didn't look back until she reached the fence. Jack wasn't far from her, his dark eyes watching her, his expression unreadable in the limited light. He still wore his leather jacket, looking like he'd stepped out of an old movie.

"I'll see you Monday." She felt like she should have said more. When he nodded, she vaulted over the fence and headed for home. She couldn't stop thinking about him standing there alone. She shouldn't feel any sympathy for him. He was a murderer and had admitted to it. But she did. He'd sounded so sad, particularly when he'd spoken of Rose.

Chapter Thirteen

Lucy

When Lucy reached home, she paused at the front door and stared at where the ink stained rosebud had been. Seeing some marks she bent closer, shining the light from her screen on the droplets of ink staining the concrete. She had no idea who had dripped ink over her rosebud. It wasn't like she had enemies. Sure, she had people she didn't get along with, but she doubted any of them would do something like that. They didn't dislike her that much. Reaching out, she ran a finger across one of the marks. It was dry. She guessed she better try and clean them off tomorrow so she didn't have to answer awkward questions from her parents when they returned Sunday. Rising to her feet, she unlocked the door and went inside.

The house was as silent as it had been earlier. Why

wasn't it more fun than this to have the house to herself? Maybe if she'd had a friend over it would have been different. Sighing, she locked the door, turned off the outside light and headed for her room. Everything was exactly as she'd left it. The window was half closed, the last of her roses were in the vase and the wastepaper bin was empty. But it didn't feel the same. Something felt different. She just didn't know what.

Spying a petal on the floor, she walked over and picked it up, rubbing the waxy object between her fingers. Obviously she hadn't placed the petals in the bin as carefully as she'd thought. Another glance around the room showed everything looked normal. Throwing the petal out she turned away from her desk and got ready for bed. She couldn't fall asleep. Every sound had her straining her ears to figure out what it was. She kept telling herself to stop being ridiculous. It wasn't like she was a little kid. She heard another sound. Was that breathing?

Sitting up, she reached out and turned on the bedside lamp. Squinting at the sudden light, she scanned the bedroom. Nothing. There was only her imagination. She was almost glad Leeah wasn't home. Her sister would have been laughing at how jumpy she was, but then again she probably wouldn't have been so jumpy if her sister had been here. Leaving the light on, she rolled over and tried to get back to sleep. It was impossible. The room was far too bright.

Dragging herself out of bed, she opened her door and turned on the hall light. About to return to her room, she saw a white rose petal on the floor. Maybe she needed a better bin. Hers was obviously useless. Picking the petal up, she stared at it. There was a single drop of red ink in the middle of the petal. Leaving her bedroom door half open, she threw the petal in the bin with the other one and crawled back into bed. Reaching out to turn off the light, she saw a smear of red on her finger. Sitting up she stared at it, surprised the ink was still wet. Grabbing a tissue, she rubbed away the mark. Shouldn't it have been dry? Or was it different when it was on a petal? The droplets on the patio had probably soaked into the concrete. She hoped not since she had no idea how to clean them off if they had.

She was tempted to have a look at the petals she'd thrown in the wheelie bin earlier, but decided she was being stupid. Everything felt odd because it was the first time she was home alone at night. She couldn't believe what a baby she was being. Sixteen-years-old and she was missing her mummy. How pathetic was that? Forcing herself to turn the bedside light off, she rolled onto her side and stared at the shadows the door created on her wall. It took ages, but eventually she fell asleep to be woken by her phone ringing, her room filled with daylight.

Sitting up properly, she tried to focus on the display of her phone. It took her several seconds to realise it was Tanner. "Morning."

Tanner chuckled. "Actually, its afternoon."

She blinked several times, trying to read the numbers on her alarm clock. "It's two o'clock?"

"Yeah. Did I wake you?"

"I can't believe it's two o'clock."

Tanner chuckled again. "And I thought I'd done well sleeping till eleven."

She scrambled out of bed, hurrying to her sister's room. It was empty. Heading back to her room, she noticed there were a couple of white petals on the floor in the hallway.

"Are you still there?"

"Yeah." She picked up the rose petals and looked around. That seemed like all of them. She was definitely getting a new bin.

"I rang to find out what movie you want to see."

"What are my choices?" She threw the petals in the bin with the other two, listening as Tanner rattled off the names of four movies. After a bit more discussion they settled on a movie and time for Tanner to collect her. When she hung up, she sent a text to Jasmine to tell her what she was going to see and what time she was leaving. She hesitated a moment then decided she definitely shouldn't tell Jasmine she'd spent her first night at home alone. Not that she had much to tell and the only interesting part she couldn't tell anyone. They'd think she was crazy.

Jasmine wasn't very good at keeping secrets and the last thing she needed was for her parents to find out she'd stayed the night alone. It wasn't like she was a little kid. She was sixteen. More than old enough to take care of herself. Some kids even moved out of home at sixteen.

She smiled at Jasmine's reply. *Ring me the moment you get home. I want to hear all about it.*

She sent a reply. *I'll tell you everything Monday. Well, some things.*

She thought she'd have more than enough time to be ready by six-thirty, when Tanner was due to pick her up. By the time she'd made breakfast, reassured her mother during an extremely lengthy conversation, replied 'no' to her sister's text asking if she was alive and washed and dried her hair, it was after six and she still hadn't decided what to wear. Her sister had also said she was staying another night at

Justin's place. That was perfectly okay with her. Now it didn't matter what time she got home.

Standing in the doorway of Leeah's room, she considered wearing her dress, but it wasn't suitable for the movies. It was more of a party kind of dress. Returning to her own room she pulled out clothes, spreading them over her bed. She alternated between shorts, a dress and jeans, finally settling on a colourful dress with thin straps and a flowing skirt. Bundling up the rest of her clothes, she dumped them in the bottom of the wardrobe. She'd nearly finished applying her make up when she heard a knock at the front door. Taking a deep breath she surveyed herself in the mirror. That had to be Tanner. She wasn't sure if she was ready. Maybe she should have put on jeans. After another deep breath, she headed for the front door.

Chapter Fourteen

Lucy

Opening the front door, Lucy found she was right. "Hi."

Tanner grinned. "You look good. Are you ready to go?"

She nodded then shook her head. "One minute. I have to grab my handbag." Leaving the door open, she dashed to her room. Grabbing her handbag, she shoved her lipstick and phone in before turning towards the door. Tanner was in the doorway. She was relieved she'd pushed all the clothes into the wardrobe and made her bed earlier. "Uhm, I'm ready."

"You don't need to say goodbye to your parents or anything?"

She shook her head, crossing the room. "No, they're not here."

Tanner stepped back to let her out of the room. "When are they home?"

She hesitated. "Tomorrow." She glanced up at Tanner in time to see him grin.

He took her hand, linking his fingers through hers. "I guess we better go or we'll miss the start of the movie."

Lucy nodded, walking to the front door with him. Leaving the outside light on, she locked the door behind her, wishing she hadn't needed to let his hand go to do so. Once they were in the car, she tried to think of something to say to him. It had been so much easier to talk to him when he was giving her a lift home after school. She glanced towards him, still trying to figure out what to say.

"Where are your parents?"

Relieved to have something to talk about, she told him about her mum's friend giving them her prize of a weekend away. She probably went into far more detail than was necessary in an effort not to let the conversation end.

They arrived at the cinema with plenty of time to buy popcorn before they made their way to their seats. Again an awkward silence fell between them and she was glad when the movie started. Barely ten minutes into the movie her phone beeped to let her know a message had come through. She nearly groaned when she saw it was from Jasmine. *You having fun? Is the movie good? Are you holding hands yet? Are you sure I have to wait till Monday to find out any details?*

She was tempted to ignore her friend, but guessed she'd probably keep sending messages until she acknowledged her. *I'll talk to you Monday. Stop messaging me. My battery is low on charge.*

Tanner bent his head close to hers. "Everything okay?"

"Yeah. It was only Jasmine."

Tanner grinned. "Was that a prearranged message in case you needed an excuse to escape a boring night?"

"No. Just Jasmine being annoying."

He laughed softly. "Are you sure? I do have a sister. I know some of the tricks she uses."

She started to object, but thought he might think she was protesting too much. Feeling slightly embarrassed, she pulled up Jasmine's message and showed it to him. "See. Jasmine being annoying." The messages were less embarrassing than him thinking she'd planned an excuse to escape his company early in case he was boring.

"Does that mean you want me to hold your hand?"

"Uhm." She returned her phone to her handbag. She had no idea what to say and on Monday she was going to tell Jasmine never to do this to her again.

Sliding his fingers between hers, he clasped her hand lightly. He leaned even closer, his lips brushing against her ear. "You don't have to wait for me to hold your hand. Go ahead and hold mine whenever you want."

She couldn't speak, wasn't even certain if she could breathe. Turning her head slightly, she met his gaze a moment before his lips met hers. By the time the movie was over, she couldn't have said what she'd watched. At the end of the movie they walked out with an arm around each other's waist. Tanner tossed the nearly full container of popcorn in the rubbish bin they passed.

Once they were in the car, Tanner asked, "Do you still have to be home by midnight?"

She thought of the silent, empty house waiting for her. "I guess not."

"There's a party on, or we could go for a drive."

"Uhm…" her voice trailed off.

"You can plug your phone into the charger if you want."

She shook her head. The battery wasn't that flat. It should last until she got home as long as she didn't have to use it for more than a few minutes. "Which did you want to do?"

"Drive. We could go to a lookout." He grinned at her.

She laughed, doubting they'd be doing much looking. "We could go back to my place for a bit."

"Are you sure?"

She nodded. "Just for a bit." The drive to her place was silent and they sat in the car when Tanner pulled up and turned off the engine. She stared out the window, once again uncertain what to say.

"You sure?"

She looked towards him, trying to see his expression in the dim interior of the car. "Yeah." Her voice was soft. "Only for a little while."

"Okay."

When he opened the car door, Lucy did too, waiting on the footpath for him as he walked around the front of the car. He reached for her hand as he stopped at her side and she returned his smile. He stood staring down at her for a minute and she wondered if she should say something.

"I'm glad you nearly ran into me on Tuesday."

She couldn't resist smiling. That had been Jack's fault. Maybe that was what she'd needed help with. She'd have to suggest it to him. She almost laughed. He'd probably be pretty disgusted to even consider the help she'd needed was his matchmaking skills, limited though they were. "I'm glad too."

Tanner stared at her for another few seconds before he walked to the front door with her, his fingers still threaded through hers. When they reached the door, he let go of her hand.

She wanted to protest. Instead, she took out her keys and unlocked the door. Her eyes were drawn to the stains on the concrete before she stepped inside. She'd forgotten all about them. She'd have to try and clean them off in the morning.

After she locked the door behind them, she led the way to her room, hanging her handbag on the bedroom door rather than open her messy wardrobe and put it away. She stopped, not far inside, trying to think of something to say to him.

Tanner nodded towards the vase. "Who are the roses from?"

"I don't know." She watched him carefully, trying to figure out if he was the one leaving them for her. She couldn't tell.

"A secret admirer?" Grinning, he crossed the distance between them.

"I guess." She met his eyes, thoughts of roses and secret admirers evaporating at the look he gave her. She reached for him at the same time as he reached for her.

Time became meaningless and Tanner ended up staying a lot longer than a bit, leaving well after midnight. She stood at the front door, waving as he left. He was completely out of sight before she could bring herself to go inside, locking the front door behind her. The silence of the house pressed in around her and she hurried to her room, grabbing her pyjamas so she could have a shower. Her pyjamas consisted of cotton shorts and a singlet, teddy bears and love hearts printed all over them. They'd been a Christmas present from Jasmine. Once she was dressed, she left the hallway light on and crawled into bed.

She lay awake, thinking about the night. Was Tanner the one leaving her roses? She still didn't know. His expression hadn't changed when he'd asked about them or when she'd answered him. She really hoped someone admitted to it soon. She was dying of curiosity. Fifteen roses and not a single clue. It was starting to get annoying. Why didn't they tell her? Pushing that from her mind, she thought about her night instead, her lips curving into a smile. Maybe Tanner would want to come over tomorrow, before her parents returned home. She'd ring him when she woke.

Chapter Fifteen

Lucy

Lucy was nearly asleep when a sound disturbed her. She lay there, trying to figure out what it was. The house was silent. She threw back the bed sheet and started to climb out of bed. The hallway light went out and she froze. A glance at the alarm clock, which sat on her bedside cabinet, showed it wasn't only the light off. There was no power at all. She stumbled out of bed and over to her door where she'd left her handbag, taking her phone out so she could use the light of her screen as a torch. She groaned when she pressed a button and the words 'Battery Low' were written on the screen. She'd forgotten all about putting it on to charge. It had been the furthest thing from her mind when Tanner had left. She guessed she better find a torch.

Still holding her phone, the screen dark again, she carefully made her way through the house. She headed for the kitchen where she was sure there was a torch in the bottom drawer. Freezing in the doorway, she stared at the figure clambering through the kitchen window and onto the bench. She guessed she must have made a sound because the shadowy figure turned towards her.

The two of them remained frozen for a moment, silhouettes in the darkened kitchen, light from the streetlight struggling to enter the window. The intruder moved first. Lucy spun, racing for the front door, her grip tightening on her phone as her heart leapt. This couldn't be happening. The first weekend she had the house to herself and someone had to break in.

Reaching the front door, it took her a moment to get it open before she raced into the night, the sound of footsteps pounding behind her. She had no idea where to go, especially barefoot and in her pyjamas. She ran down the centre of the road, the bitumen beneath her feet feeling like it was cutting into her. Behind she could still hear footsteps. They kept time with the beat of her heart, seeming to grow closer.

When she realised she was heading in the direction of the school, she thought of Jack. Was this it? Was this what he needed to help her with? The intruder continued to chase after her, only the sound of his feet letting her know he was there. Why didn't he say something? Yell or call out to her. Anything. It seemed worse that he ran after her not saying a word. And where was everyone? Friday night there'd been people about. Not many, but a few. Ones she could have run to and begged for help. Tonight there seemed to be none. Although it was much later than she'd been out last night. If it could still be considered night since it was more than likely around two a.m. Sunday morning. Then she wondered why she was even thinking about the time. All she should be worried about was escaping.

Ahead of her she could see the fence and she veered towards the footpath, calling Jack's name under her breath. A second later he appeared at the fence, an indistinct figure in the night. She tried to run faster, but couldn't. Even when Jack called her name, urging her to hurry, she still couldn't go any faster.

Just before she reached the footpath her pursuer tackled her, his arms going around her waist. She sprawled across the road, feeling gravel cut into her hands and knees. She struggled to escape, but he refused to let her go, grunting as her elbow caught him in the face.

"Lucy! Come on, Lucy. I can't help you while you're out there. I can't leave the school grounds," Jack said.

She wriggled out of the arms holding her, kicking out at him as she scrambled to her feet, racing to the fence. She grabbed hold of the top of the fence to pull herself over when a body slammed into her, trying to tackle her to the ground.

Jack clasped her hands firmly, pulling her towards him. "I don't know how to help you fight him. Only you can see and touch me."

She twisted and turned trying to break free as she clung to Jack's hands, kicking at the person who held her. He grunted and loosened his grip. "Pull me over the fence, Jack." She cried out in pain as Jack dragged her over the fence, landing sprawled on top of him. Even though he broke her fall, her hands hit the ground, dirt and sticks making the grazes on her hands hurt even more.

"Get up. Hurry. He's getting over the fence." Jack pushed her off him, helping her rise. He held her hand tightly, racing through the trees towards the school buildings.

"Where are we going?" She checked over her shoulder to see if she was still being followed. What did he want? Why couldn't he leave her alone? She didn't care if he stole the television. He could take her laptop too for all she cared. Just as long as he left her alone.

"We might be able to lose him amongst the buildings."

Another glance behind her showed the pursuer wasn't close enough to hear her words if she kept her voice low. "I can't keep running. My legs are aching, I've got a stitch in my side and my hands and knees are grazed and bleeding."

"Do you want him to catch you? Who is it? Do you know him?"

"I wouldn't have a clue. There hasn't been enough light to see him, but I doubt I know him. It's just some stranger who broke into my home."

"This way." Jack abruptly changed direction.

"Can't you do anything?"

"I'm a ghost, Lucy. There's not much I can do. But I know this school, including every place to hide if we can lose him for a minute."

She glanced behind, relieved to see more distance between her and her pursuer. Maybe they could lose him long enough for her to hide. "Why go this way?"

"So we can see him. There's a light that's always on near the main entrance."

She didn't know how that was going to help, but

didn't bother asking. She was now barely able to breathe let alone continue to hold a conversation. She glanced down at the phone in her hand as she kept running. There wasn't enough charge to make a call, but she should be able to send a text message to her sister if she could get a few seconds to type it.

She looked around. Here probably wasn't the best place to try. Not with all the buildings to run into, but unless she could lose her pursuer there probably wasn't going to be a better time. "Don't let me run into anything." She started to type in the message, one handed. It was painstakingly slow as she glanced between the screen and where they were going.

"What are you doing?" Jack asked.

"Sending my sister a message that I need help." She stumbled.

"Be careful."

She didn't bother answering. Breathing was more important. She finally finished typing the message and sent it. *Battery low. At school. Being chased. Call police.* Now she had to hope her sister was awake and took her seriously.

Chapter Sixteen

Lucy

Ahead of her she could see the light Jack had mentioned. A look over her shoulder showed her pursuer was keeping up. He'd dropped behind slightly, but not enough for her to be able to hide.

Then she was reaching the light and running past it, glancing back when she thought he might be in it. She came to a sudden stop, only remaining on her feet because of Jack. "Dylan?" Surely not, but there he stood, also stopping suddenly. "Why?"

"I thought you saw me. In the kitchen. You didn't?"

She shook her head.

"Forget about talking to him. You need to hide until your sister can send help." Jack tugged on her hand.

She ignored Jack. "Why?"

"You'll tell. I didn't mean for you to know I was there. I just wanted to leave another rose for you. I'm sorry about the ink. I shouldn't have got mad about your boyfriend. I thought you liked me. You said the roses were sweet and romantic."

"You gave them to me?" She slowly shook her head, not wanting to believe it was Dylan. He was the last person she wanted roses from. She thought of Cole. Well, one of the last people.

"Come on." Jack tugged on her hand again. "Run while he's confused. Just because you know him doesn't mean he won't hurt you."

While Jack was still talking, Dylan said, "I thought you liked me. Every time I came over with Justin you sat with me and talked to me."

She was going to kill her sister. "He's not going to hurt me, Jack." She turned to Dylan. "I was being polite." Maybe she should tell Cole to quit staring at her. Just in case.

"Who are you talking to?" Dylan looked in the direction she'd spoken. "There's no one there. Who's Jack?"

"Go home, Dylan."

"And you won't tell anyone? I can visit you Monday afternoon when Justin visits Leeah."

"You've got to be kidding me." The words exploded from her.

"Shut up. Let him think what he wants," Jack said.

"You can't tell. You have to promise not to tell." Dylan took a step towards her.

Lucy backed away.

"Tell him you won't. Promise whatever he wants to hear. Whatever it takes to get rid of him," Jack said.

"Okay. I won't tell. I'm sure you won't do it again." She took a step away from him. "And I'll see you Monday afternoon."

"You will?" Dylan sounded surprised. "What about your boyfriend?"

"Uhm." She tried to think what to say.

"Tell him you're over."

She repeated Jack's words.

"You are?" Dylan continued to sound surprised. "But he didn't leave until after midnight."

"You let Tanner stay when no one else was at home with you?" Jack asked.

She glared at Jack, not impressed with his tone. "You're not helping, Jack. Aren't you meant to be helping? Besides, it's none of your business."

"Who are you talking to?" Dylan asked.

"Stop talking to me," Jack said. "It makes you look

crazy. Although I'm surprised he even notices since he's probably completely out of his tree."

She ignored Jack, answering Dylan instead. "My imaginary friend."

Dylan stared at her for a moment. "You don't mean anything you just said. You're going to tell, aren't you? And I haven't had an imaginary friend since I was nine. I was only a kid. It's okay for a kid to have an imaginary friend."

She nearly groaned, but stopped herself at the last moment. It wouldn't help, only make it harder to undo her mistake. "I didn't mean it. Jack isn't exactly an imaginary friend. He's a ghost."

"There's no such thing as a ghost."

"How can you be sure?"

"They're not real."

She took a step backwards. "Just because you've never seen one, doesn't mean they're not real."

"This isn't helping," Jack said. "I don't know what you thought would happen by telling him this, but he doesn't seem to be falling for it."

She didn't have a clue, but she had to try something. She couldn't continue to run all night. "He's standing here beside me." She raised her hand that still clasped hold of Jack's. "I'm holding his hand right now. And I'm the only one who can see him, hear him or touch him."

"Why are you the only one? What makes you so different?"

"I don't know." She moved back slightly. "I saw him for the first time on Monday."

"Why then?"

She shrugged, taking another half step back. "I wouldn't have a clue." Telling him that Jack had more than likely appeared so he could help her deal with him probably wasn't a good idea. "If you want to ask him a question, I could tell you what he says." She took another half a step away from Dylan. If she could just keep him distracted long enough for help to arrive. She glanced at her phone she still clutched in her other hand, wondering if she should check the time. No, that might have him wondering what she was waiting for.

"Why is he a ghost?"

"Can he be any more unoriginal? You probably shouldn't tell him it's because I killed two people. You don't want to give him any ideas," Jack said.

"What's he saying?" Dylan asked.

"Tell him it's because I'm dead."

She repeated Jack's last words.

"I knew you were stringing me along." Dylan strode towards her.

Chapter Seventeen

Lucy

Lucy backed away, shaking her head. "I'm not. He's really here. He also isn't very amusing, even though he thinks he is. Ask him another question." She tried not to speak too fast, but she wasn't very successful. She sounded afraid and Dylan would have to be a complete idiot if he didn't realise. He continued to advance on her and she kept retreating. Why hadn't her sister sent help yet?

"When did he die?"

"Friday the first of March, 1963. On my eighteenth birthday."

She glanced towards Jack as she repeated his words. "Ask him something else, Dylan. Isn't there anything else you want to know?"

"Why can't I see him? If he's really there, other people should be able to see him."

She nearly growled in frustration. He was difficult to distract. She also wished he'd stop walking towards her. "I don't know. Ask him a question. Don't you want to ask him a question? I mean, how often do you get the chance to talk to a ghost?"

"How did he die?"

"Great. He would have to ask that. It's probably another question you shouldn't tell him the answer to. If he hears my girlfriend stabbed me he might wonder what you're planning. Tell him I had a motorcycle accident. He won't know it's a lie."

When she told him, Dylan asked, "Why is he here? Don't ghosts have to haunt where they died?"

"Because he died here," Lucy said. She barely managed not to tell him to stop moving. A glance around the area showed they were still alone. Wasn't anyone coming?

"What sort of bike was it?"

"How about we skip all the questions and just make another run for it?" Jack asked.

"Come on Jack, answer the question."

"I knew it. It's all a lie," Dylan said. "You don't have a clue what sort of bike someone would own in sixty-three."

"Tell him it was a 1953 Royal Enfield Bullet."

She hurriedly repeated Jack's words.

Dylan came to a complete stop. "He's real? There's a ghost standing beside you?"

"Run," Jack ordered.

She didn't need to be told twice. Letting Jack lead the way she ran, not looking back to see if Dylan followed. They headed around the side of one of the buildings, stopping at the back.

"You can climb up on the roof from here." Jack looked behind them. "Hurry, before he follows."

She tucked her phone into the side of her pyjama shorts and with Jack's help clambered up the side of the building using a window ledge and a downpipe. As soon as she was on the roof, she lay down flat, peering over the edge. She still couldn't see Dylan.

Jack joined her. "He's just started moving. Keeping him talking wasn't such a crazy idea after all."

Lucy didn't say anything. She didn't want to risk Dylan hearing her. She could finally see him, walking towards the building she was on top of. As he came closer, she held her breath, mentally begging him to keep walking. He had nearly gone completely past the building when her phone rang.

She grabbed her phone and, seeing it was her sister,

pressed the answer button. Leeah started speaking before she even had a chance to say hello.

"This better not be a jo-" The phone went dead.

"Lucy? Where are you? I know you're around here. I heard your phone." Dylan slowly turned on the spot.

Lucy momentarily closed her eyes, tucking her phone back into the waistband of her pyjama shorts. She didn't have a clue what to do. If she moved, he'd definitely see her. Surely if she stayed still he wouldn't think to look on the roof.

"Keep your head down," Jack said.

She pressed her cheek against the roof, the bumpy corrugations uncomfortable and cold against her body. Lying on a roof at the beginning of March in the early hours of the morning wearing thin cotton pyjamas wasn't her idea of fun. So much for a weekend without parents. It had been a complete fail. She thought of going to the movies with Tanner and coming back to her place afterwards. Okay, so maybe not a complete fail.

"Lucy!"

She remained pressed against the roof. Why couldn't he go home and leave her alone? What did he plan to do? How did he think he was going to stop her from talking? She shuddered as only bad scenarios came to mind.

"Come out, Lucy. I just want to talk to you. Explain things. Make sure you understand."

"Don't even think about moving." Jack rose to his feet and looked over the edge. "He's almost directly below you."

She wasn't an idiot. There was no way she was going down there to talk to Dylan. She ignored him as he continued to plead with her.

Jack sat back beside her. "I wish he'd shut up. He's really starting to bug me. Someone needs to deck him."

"Lucy!"

That had been Leeah's voice. She started to sit up, but Jack pressed her down. "That's Leeah. I have to go down there." She kept her voice low, not wanting to catch Dylan's attention. "I'm not about to leave her alone with him."

"Don't be a ditz. If you go down there, he's going to hurt you."

"So I should let him hurt my sister instead?" She rolled away from Jack, peering over the edge. "Not going to happen."

"Lucy? If you're here you better hurry up and

answer me before I go home. If this is your idea of a joke, I'm going to make you regret it."

Leeah was coming closer and the last thing she wanted was to have Dylan hurt her. "I'm over here."

"Where?" Leeah called out.

"You called your sister?" Dylan asked from below. "You told her?"

"Over here." Lucy rose to her feet.

"This is worse than playing Marco Polo," Leeah shouted.

Before Lucy could reply, Jack pulled her back from the edge. She started to demand what he was doing when she saw Dylan's hand on the edge of the roof, soon followed by his body.

"You told. You promised not to tell."

Chapter Eighteen

Lucy

Lucy backed away from Dylan, ignoring her sister who was calling out to her. "It was before I promised. I sent her a text."

"Now I'm going to be in trouble again and it's all your fault."

"No it's not." She had not started this and she wasn't about to take the blame.

"Don't argue with him. Tell him what he wants to hear," Jack said. "Focus on getting out of this alive."

"I mean, no you're not. I'm sure we can sort this out." She was tempted to tell her sister to shut up, but didn't want to say anything that might set Dylan off. "I liked the roses. They were very pretty." She took a step backwards, feeling with her bare feet where to step. She stumbled as she passed the peak of the roof.

"You did? You really liked them?"

"Lucy? What are you doing up there? Who's that with you?" Leeah stared up at her.

"Dylan? What are you doing here?" Justin asked.

Dylan shook his head, muttering 'no' under his breath over and over again. Occasionally he said 'you promised'.

Lucy took a step to the side, planning to go around him so she could climb off the roof. She hadn't even finished taking a single step when Dylan barrelled into her. She heard her sister scream and herself echoing her.

"Fight him, don't let him push you over the edge." Jack ran after her to stand between her and the edge of the roof.

"I'm trying." She struggled against Dylan, feeling herself getting closer and closer to the edge by the second. In the background she could hear Leeah and Justin yelling and Leeah demanding he do something.

"Lucy, come on. You're inches from the edge. Fight harder."

"I can't." The words came out sounding like a sob. "Jack, help me." Her leg slipped over the edge. "Dylan. Let me go. Please let me go." She felt Jack land on her, his weight pressing her away from the edge.

"Don't fight me. I won't let you go over," Jack said. "Give me your hand."

She let Jack's hand wrap around hers, turning it into a fist. Then she was punching Dylan in the jaw, with the help of Jack. Dylan's grip loosened and they hit him again.

Jack dragged her away from Dylan and towards the middle of the roof. "Are you hurt?"

She shook her head, looking at Dylan who remained lying on the roof, curled into a ball as he cradled his jaw with his hand. Walking unsteadily to the edge of the roof, she stared at her sister who was arguing with Justin. It took a moment for their words to sink in. "No. Absolutely no." She clambered down off the roof and strode to her sister's side. "Are you crazy?" She glared at Justin.

"You don't understand," Justin said.

"No. You don't understand. Your brother broke into my house tonight... this morning. That isn't right. You can't enter people's houses without their permission."

"Why didn't you ring me?" Leeah demanded.

"I tried. My battery was flat." She realised her phone was missing. "And I have no idea where it is right now, but if it had been charged I would have called the police."

"It's on the roof," Jack said.

She started to thank him then remembered no one else could hear him. It had been okay to talk to him in front of Dylan, but the last thing she needed was for her sister to think she'd lost the plot. "Call the police, Leeah."

"I can't let you," Justin said.

"You'd side with your brother instead of me?" Leeah demanded.

Justin shrugged. "He's my brother."

Lucy stepped between Leeah and Justin. "Call the police, Leeah."

"Do you really think you're a match for me?" Justin laughed. "Really?"

She probably wasn't, but all she had to do was buy some time for her sister to make the call.

"What do you think you're doing, Lucy? Run," Jack ordered.

"Leeah. Run. Ring the cops." She threw herself at Justin, tackling him to the ground. Probably only managing because he wasn't expecting the move. She swore as his fist connected with her jaw and she wondered if this was how Dylan had felt.

"Fight him," Jack said. "Come on, Lucy. You can do better than this."

She wanted to say she couldn't, but she was too busy trying not to have her face smashed in. She was even too busy to ask Jack for help.

Jack continued to stand over her. "Are you trying to get yourself killed? Fight him. Don't you know how to fight?"

"You're going to call your sister back." Justin held her pinned to the ground leaning over her. "They're not putting my brother in hospital again. He said he'd kill himself if they did. That's not going to happen."

"No." She answered both of them, but wasn't sure if Jack realised that. "I don't know how, Jack."

"It's Justin, not Jack. And it's simple. Call her name. She'll come."

Dylan appeared behind his brother and stared down at Lucy. "She's talking to a ghost."

Panic hit Lucy and she tried to remain calm. There was no way she could fight off the two of them. When she saw Leeah behind Dylan, a branch drawn back to swing at him, she tried to think of a way to distract him. "Ghosts aren't real. Don't tell me you believe in them, Dylan."

"They are! You told me they are." Dylan pointed his finger at her, yelling the words.

Leeah swung the branch. A cracking sound caused them all to fall silent as Dylan crashed to the ground.

Justin was the first to move, roaring as he started shaking Lucy, her head connecting with the ground.

Leeah screamed, trying to pull Justin away from her.

Jack grabbed hold of her hand. "Let me in. Say yes, Lucy."

The world spun around her and her head ached from where it had connected with the ground. "Yes." Then it felt like her body was crowded and far too small, controlled by someone other than herself. Her fist connected with Justin's jaw, but he didn't loosen his grip. Blow after blow was rained upon him, until she was finally breaking free of him. He rose to his feet, swinging a fist towards her face. She ducked, sinking her fist into his stomach, sweeping his legs out from under him by hooking her right ankle around his. Justin crashed to the ground and she reached forward, grabbing him by the shirt, smashing her fist into his face. Letting go of his shirt she watched as he dropped back to the ground.

Then she felt empty, Jack standing in front of her, his hands on her shoulders as he asked if she was all right. She shook her head, then nodded, not sure what to tell him. Behind her Leeah was sobbing and she could hear sirens. Jack started to fade. "Don't go." Her words were a whisper.

Jack smiled, drawing away from her. "I guess we figured out what you needed help with after all."

He disappeared and she hoped he was still there so he could hear her whispered words. "Thank you, Jack."

Leeah took a couple of hesitant steps towards her. "What happened to you? It was like you were possessed. I know you can't fight."

Lucy crossed the distance between them, taking hold of her sister's hand, wincing at the pain not only in her hands, but most of her body. "What are we going to tell Mum and Dad?"

Leeah started to laugh, tears continuing to fall. "We are so dead."

She had to agree. Their parents would probably ground them for life. Dylan groaned and her eyes were drawn to him. She hoped the police arrived before he regained consciousness. Although she guessed that since Jack was gone they were probably safe. "You'll have to ring them. My phone is flat and up on the roof."

They were still arguing over who had to ring their parents when the police found them.

Chapter Nineteen

Jack

Jack sat in the groundsman's shed, leaning against the wall with his leg drawn up to rest his arm on, staring at the back of the old wardrobe.

It was Wednesday morning and Lucy hadn't been at school the past two days. He'd wandered around hoping to catch someone gossiping about what had happened, but it looked like no one had been told. Or if they had, they weren't talking about it. Not even her friend Jasmine. Hopefully she'd be here today. He knew he wouldn't be able to talk to her and she wouldn't be able to see or hear him, but at least he could see if she was okay.

When he'd asked her to let him in Sunday morning he hadn't known for certain if it'd work. The day he'd walked through Jasmine he'd felt like he could have easily taken over her body. He'd never felt that before. Things were obviously different now. Although he was sure that taking over someone's body without their permission would only give him another sin to atone for. He already had far too many without adding more.

"Jack?"

His name was spoken softly, but he recognised the voice. Rising to his feet, he walked through the wardrobe and the rest of the clutter filling the groundsman's shed. He stopped out the front of the building, his eyes checking over Lucy. There was a dark bruise on her jaw and scratches and bruises visible on the rest of her body.

"Are you here, Jack?" She remained silent a moment. "I don't suppose you could open the door or something and let me know if you're here."

He wished he could ask her how she was and what had happened once the police had taken them away Sunday morning.

"Jack?" She sounded uncertain.

He stepped backwards through the locked door, trying to force it to open. The door stayed closed. Anger rushed through him. That blasted bird could have given him long enough to say goodbye properly. He stepped forward again and the door flew open.

"Jack." There was relief in her voice this time. She stepped inside, using her phone to shine the way. "It feels really odd talking to someone I can't see or hear." She slowly turned as if searching for him. "I wanted to say thank you. And let you know what happened."

He followed her as she wove her way through the clutter and slipped between the wall and the old wardrobe. He watched her as she continued to stand there, shifting from one foot to the other.

"Dylan is getting help and Justin is looking at time in jail." She smiled momentarily. "Leeah ditched him." She sobered. "Mum and Dad weren't impressed. We're both grounded. Leeah argued about it because she doesn't think she should be grounded at eighteen. Mum said she shouldn't have needed to ground her. That she should have been more responsible." She fell silent again. "Are you still here?" She paused. "I looked up some old newspaper stories from when you died."

When she fell silent, and remained that way, Jack wished he could tell her to hurry up and tell him what she wanted to say.

"I'm sorry. About everything that happened to you. About your mum. All of it." Again she fell silent.

"I remembered what you said about missing Rose." She swung her schoolbag off her back and onto the floor, crouching in front of it to rummage inside. "I brought a picture of her for you. It's just a photocopy. I thought I could blu tac it to the wall." She looked around the space. "I wish you could tell me yes or no. I don't want to put it up if you don't want it."

"Put the picture up, Lucy." He knew she couldn't hear him, but he couldn't stop himself from speaking the words. He moved to stand directly in front of her. "Please, Lucy." She held the picture up and it was right in front of his eyes. He found himself staring at Rose's smiling face. Pain arrowed through him and he reached for the picture, wanting to touch it.

"Jack? Are you still here?"

"Yes." His hand brushed through the picture, unable to touch. He closed his eyes, tilting his head back as he took a deep breath. Opening his eyes he was in time to see Lucy walk through him.

She stopped, turning around to face him. "Jack?"

"Put the picture up. Come on, Lucy." Again he reached for the picture. This time it moved slightly.

Lucy grinned. "I'll take that as a yes." She turned to face the wall, pressing blu tac into each corner before she put the picture up, just above her eye height. Turning, she stepped to the side, leaning against the wall. "There's so much I want to tell you. Tanner dropped in to see me Monday afternoon when I didn't go to school. I told him what had happened. He couldn't ring me because my phone was broken in the fight. I only got a new one yesterday. Mum wouldn't let me go to school until I had one. She's also making Leeah and me take self-defence classes."

Even though he listened to what she had to say, he couldn't keep his eyes off Rose's picture.

"She doesn't want to let me out of her sight and wanted to take time off work to look after me. It would have driven me crazy to have her hovering over me twenty-four seven." She fell silent. "I wish I could see you one last time so I can thank you properly. I'm sorry life happened to you, as you put it. And I'm glad you were there so Dylan didn't end up killing me. Or whatever he'd planned to do so I couldn't tell anyone."

She fell silent long enough that Jack thought she might be finished. He dragged his eyes away from the picture to stare at her, stepping in front of her so he could gaze into the eyes that couldn't see him.

"I wish someone had been there to help you when you'd needed it."

When she walked through him, he turned to watch

her squeeze between the wall and the wardrobe. "So do I, Lucy. So do I."

Free Ebook

Subscribe to Avril's newsletter to receive a free ebook. This ebook is exclusive to those on her mailing list. To find out more about this offer visit:

www.avrilsabine.com/free-ebook

*

Acknowledgements

Thank you to everyone involved in getting this story finished. Particularly Mum and Cat for being so demanding and making sure this story improved dramatically.

To The Reader

If you enjoyed this book, why not consider leaving a review to help other readers discover it too? Reader engagement is one of the few ways that lets an author know readers want more books in a particular series or genre. So leave a review and tell friends, not only about this book but also about other ones you've enjoyed, so you can continue to enjoy books by your favourite authors for years to come.

Dreams are meant to be lived,

Avril.

About The Author

Avril is an Australian author who lives with her family on acreage in South East Queensland. She writes mostly young adult speculative fiction, but has been known to dabble in other genres. You can find more information about her at her website www.avrilsabine.com where you can also subscribe to her newsletter to be kept informed about new releases, current projects, blog posts and exclusive news.

Titles By Avril Sabine

Stories about strong characters and characters who discover their strengths.

SERIES

Assassins Of The Dead- Young Adult Fantasy/ Paranormal

Book 1: Dark Blade

Book 2: Dragon Touched

Dragon Blood- Young Adult Urban Fantasy (with elements of romance)

(5 book series)

Book 1: Pliethin

Book 2: Wyvern

Book 3: Surety

Book 4: Knight

Book 5: Mage

Dragon Mage- Young Adult Urban Fantasy (with elements of romance)

(Series two of Dragon Blood series)

Book 1: Promise

Dragon Blood Chronicles- Young Adult Urban Fantasy (with elements of romance)

(Companion stand alone series to Dragon Blood)

Book 1: Oath

Book 2: Betrayed

Guardians Of The Round Table- Young Adult Fantasy LitRPG

(Co-written with Storm and Rhys Petersen)

Book 1: Dexterity Fail

Book 2: Goblin Boots

Book 3: Singed Feathers

Book 4: Frog Mage

Book 5: Crystal Mine

Book 6: Cursed Harp

Rosie's Rangers- Young Adult Western Steampunk

(6 book series)

Book 1: Justice

Book 2: Vengeance

Book 3: Treachery

Book 4: Accused

Book 5: Wanted

Book 6: Corruption

Mark Of Kings- Children's Fantasy

(Upper middle grade/preteen)

(4 book series)

Book 1: The Arena

Book 2: The Island

Book 3: The Assassin

Book 4: The King

STAND ALONE SERIES

Demon Hunters- Young Adult Urban Fantasy/ Horror (with elements of romance)

Book 1: Blood Sacrifice

Book 2: Retribution

Book 3: Tainted

Book 4: Premonition

Book 5: Cursed

Book 6: Feud

Book 7: Extrication

Plea Of The Damned- Young Adult Urban Fantasy/Paranormal

(6 book series)

Book 1: Forgive Me Lucy

Book 2: Forgive Me Aiden

Book 3: Forgive Me Jena

Book 4: Forgive Me Kobe

Book 5: Forgive Me Marti

Book 6: Forgive Me Dawson

***Realms Of The Fae- Young Adult Urban Fantasy
(with elements of romance)***

The Sword (short story in Like A Girl Anthology)

Heart Of Stone

Book 1: A Debt Owed

Book 2: Marked By The Hunt

Book 3: The Magic Collector

Book 4: An Unexpected Betrayal

Book 5: Imprisoned By Iron

Fairytales Retold (Short Stories)

Snow-White And Rose-Red

The Twelve Brothers

The Light Princess

Beauty And The Beast

Sleeping Beauty

Aschenputtel

The Golden Bird

The Frog Prince

The Death Of Koshchei The Deathless

Myths And Legends Retold (Short Stories)

Ion, Son Of Apollo

Sir Gawain And The Maid With The Narrow Sleeves

Princess Ilse, The Giant's Daughter

YOUNG ADULT NOVELS

Young Adult Fantasy (with elements of romance)

Elf Sight

Earth Bound

Young Adult Urban Fantasy

Stone Warrior (with elements of romance)

The Jungle Inside

Young Adult Contemporary (with elements of romance)

Through Your Eyes

The Ugly Stepsister

Perfect Little Princess

Young Adult Contemporary/Paranormal

Whispers In The Dark (with elements of romance and same sex relationships)

Over Too Soon (with elements of romance)

Young Adult Sci-Fi

Experiment X-One-Six (Urban Sci-Fi/Superheroes)

An Endless Dawn (Post Apocalyptic Sci-Fi)

CHILDREN'S BOOKS

Dragon Lord (Preteen/early teens) (Fantasy)

The Irish Wizard (Upper middle grade) (Urban Fantasy)

SHORT STORIES

Urban Fantasy

Eternally Late

Dealings With Joe

Glimpses (short story in That Moment When Anthology)

Contemporary

The Brat Next Door

Fantasy LitRPG

(Set in the same world as Guardians Of The Round Table Series)

Tales Of Inadon 1: The Disc (Co-written with Storm and Rhys Petersen) (short story in Game On! Anthology)

Post Apocalyptic Sci-Fi

Compulsive Directive

NONFICTION

A Year Of Weekly Writing Exercises (Creative Writing)

Cooking For Families With Allergies (Cooking) (Co-written with Storm Petersen)

Tell Me A Story, Grandma (Memoir)

ONLINE COURSE

Overview Of Independently Publishing A Book

For the most up to date details on available titles visit:

www.avrilsabine.com/books/bibliography

Plea Of The Damned Series

To learn more about this series visit:

www.avrilsabine.com/series/potd

**BOOKS AVAILABLE IN THE PLEA OF THE
DAMNED SERIES:**

Book 1: Forgive Me Lucy

Book 2: Forgive Me Aiden

Book 3: Forgive Me Jena

Book 4: Forgive Me Kobe

Book 5: Forgive Me Marti

Book 6: Forgive Me Dawson

Disclaimer

are either the products of the author's imagination or used in a fictitious manner. Any resemblance to actual persons, living or dead, or actual events is purely coincidental. The opinions expressed or beliefs held are those of the characters and should not be assumed to be the opinions or beliefs of the author.